"Bewitching," he murmured just before his mouth claimed hers. He kissed her gently at first, and though he held her securely, he was ready to release her the instant she protested. Instead, she surprised him with the sweetness of her lips, returning his kiss with a generosity that sent the fire surging through him. He deepened the kiss, tumbling them both into a world neither had dreamed of.

Candace pressed against him, yearning to be as close as possible, thrilling to the waves of pleasure his kisses evoked. . . .

By Jeanne Carmichael
Published by Fawcett Books:

LORD OF THE MANOR
LADY SCOUNDREL
A BREATH OF SCANDAL

A BREATH OF SCANDAL

Jeanne Carmichael

FAWCETT CREST • NEW YORK

A Fawcett Crest Book
Published by Ballantine Books
Copyright © 1995 by Carol Quinto

All rights reserved under International and Pan-American Copyright Conventions. Published in the United States by Ballantine Books, a division of Random House, Inc., New York, and simultaneously in Canada by Random House of Canada Limited, Toronto.

Library of Congress Catalog Card Number: 95-90345

ISBN 0-449-22372-8

Manufactured in the United States of America

First Edition: September 1995

10 9 8 7 6 5 4 3 2 1

Prologue

Damian Edward Croyden Reynald, the sixth Earl of Doncaster, returned from a tour of Deerpark, his principal residence, weary of listening to the arguments between Brownlow, his estate manager, and John Siddons, his secretary, which had raged between the two for the better part of the day.

Damian seldom approached the courtyard without being moved by the sheer beauty of the old house—the warmth of the stone walls, the flaming creeper climbing the gate house tower, the large mullioned windows with the afternoon sun glinting on the square panes, the still moat full now of water lilies and one lone swan swimming majestically—but now he barely glanced at his home, and found no comfort in his surroundings.

Deerpark had come to him on the death of his father, four years before. Damian had been four-and-twenty then, a tall young man with thick black hair that fell in natural waves across his forehead, and matched the color of the heavy eyebrows above wide-set eyes—eyes that appeared dark brown when he was in good humor, and nearly black when he was angry or tired. His eyes were black now as he gazed at his retainers. He was tired of listening to their bickering, tired of the responsibilities he'd

1

assumed, and tired of worrying about his younger brother.

"My lord, I think you should reconsider such extensive repairs," Siddons protested. "Beers is the least productive of all your tenant farmers—"

"Which has nothing to do with the matter," Brownlow interrupted. "The work needs to be done, and may I remind you, maintaining his lordship's property is my business—"

"And seeing to his finances is mine—"

"Enough, the pair of you," Damian ordered curtly. "I shall give you my decision in the morning." It said much for his self-control that he did not lash out further, for his head ached abominably and he had other worries to contend with besides the renovations his tenants had requested. At the moment, he wanted only a few moments of quiet and something cool to drink.

He realized he was likely to get neither as he observed a lavishly trimmed town coach in the yard, the gilded crest on the door and boot indicating a visitor of some rank. They were not, to his knowledge, expecting any guests, and the equipage did not look familiar.

Dismounting in the courtyard, he tossed his reins to a stable lad who came running, and strode into the house through the tall casement windows of a small salon situated near the grand staircase. If his stepmother was entertaining guests, he could slip up to his bedchamber unseen and change his riding dress before presenting himself.

But Creswall, the tall white-haired butler who had been at Deerpark longer than Damian could remember, intercepted him in the hall. "Good afternoon, my lord. Lady Doncaster requests you join her as soon as possible."

Damian nodded as he started up the stairs. "Thank you. Tell her I shall be down directly."

Creswall coughed discreetly. "Beggin' your pardon, my lord, but I believe her ladyship would prefer you come at once. His Grace, the Duke of Cardiff, is with her in the south drawing room."

Damian halted on the steps, idly tapping the riding crop he carried against his skintight buff pantaloons as he considered the situation. Cardiff was the last person he expected to see at Deerpark. To say that they were not on terms was an understatement. The last time Damian had encountered him, two years before, the duke had threatened to have him horsewhipped for daring to thwart his plans.

Damian smiled coldly, recalling the incident. He had attended the theater and stayed afterward, waiting for Sally Richmond, one of the leading actresses, to join him for a late supper. As he was escorting the lady to her carriage, he'd heard a young girl crying out for help in the alleyway behind the theater and, despite Sally's warnings, had gone to her rescue.

The girl, Lily, was no more than a child really, and she had been frightened badly when Cardiff tried to force her into his carriage. Damian handed her over to Sally, and then suggested quietly that His Grace find someone more receptive to his advances.

The duke had been furious. Damian could still remember the insane fury in the man's eyes, and his blustering manner. But he'd backed down quickly enough when Damian offered to meet him, when and where the duke chose. However, His Grace was not the sort to face a man honorably, and had Sally and a few others not been present, he would have likely drawn his pistol then and there.

But there were witnesses, and Damian had managed to walk off with the girl unharmed. Lily, sobbing against Sally's shoulder in the carriage, had wanted only to return to her home in the north. Respecting her wishes, Damian had spirited her out of London, and provided enough funds to see her safely home. Sally warned him that he had not heard the last of the affair. Cardiff had been made to look foolish, and he would not likely forgive or forget that.

Damian knew she was right. He'd crossed paths with the duke on a few occasions since, and though both had behaved civilly, the animosity between them was apparent enough that bets had been laid at White's on the outcome of their quarrel.

And now the duke was at Deerpark.

Damian came slowly down the steps. "In the south drawing room, did you say?"

"Yes, my lord."

Damian strolled unhurriedly down the long tiled hall. The double doors leading into the drawing room stood open, and he nodded to one of his footmen standing attentively in the hall before he stepped quietly through the doors. He took a moment to survey the scene.

Louisa, the Dowager Countess of Doncaster, was seated on the brocaded sofa near the windows. She had the same blond hair and blue eyes as her younger son, but not his height. Despite her lack of inches, she possessed a regal air, and to those who did not know of her kind heart and sentimental nature, she often seemed forbidding.

Opposite her, in a tall wing chair, the Duke of Cardiff sat at his ease. He had gained weight since Damian saw him last, and his face had taken on the florid countenance of a man addicted to drink. The small dark eyes Damian remembered were red-veined, but just as cold.

Louisa glanced up and caught sight of him. "Dearest," she cried, rising and extending her hands. "The Duke of Cardiff has honored us with a visit."

Damian crossed the room and took her hands in his. He could feel their cold trembling, and wondered what Cardiff had said to upset her. Anger burned in him, but he turned and greeted their guest with tolerable composure. "I regret I was not at home to receive you, Your Grace. To what do we owe this visit? Somehow, I feel certain it is not merely because you seek the pleasure of my company."

"Oh, I always find you amusing, Doncaster, however, 'tis business I wish to discuss. Perhaps your lovely stepmother will excuse us?"

Louisa looked to her son for guidance, her blue eyes clouded with concern.

Damian nodded. As she took her leave of them, he strode to the sideboard and poured a brandy. Quite deliberately, he did not offer a glass to his guest.

The duke appeared not to notice. "Lady Doncaster is still a beautiful woman. It pains me to think I may be the bearer of sad news for her."

"Shall we dispense with the pleasantries, Cardiff? What is it you want?"

5

"Ah, you were always so gracious, Doncaster, but perhaps in this instance you are right. I came here seeking your brother, and discovered he has not been seen in a month."

"Harry will be touched by your concern."

The duke reddened but retained his temper: He withdrew a folded note from his purse and tossed it on the table. "A fortnight ago your foolish brother challenged me to a game of piquet, apparently under the illusion that he was adept at cards. It distresses me to tell you that he lost to the tune of sixty thousand pounds—which he pledged to make good within a day or two. Assuming him to be a gentleman, I, of course, accepted his word."

"Harry played cards with you? Somehow, I find that rather difficult to believe. I know my brother to be lacking in judgment, but—"

"Careful, Doncaster. You will go too far one of these days, and it will give me great pleasure to teach you a lesson in manners. For the moment, however, I am more concerned with your brother."

"You need not be. If indeed Harry lost to you, you may rest assured he will make good his vowel."

"Your confidence in your brother is touching, my lord, but I cannot share it. The debt is vastly overdue, and Harry seems to have disappeared. I fear he wagered over his head, and now will not face the consequences."

Damian restrained his temper, but the lines of his jaw hardened and his eyes darkened ominously. "What are you implying, Cardiff?"

The duke rose to his full height. He stood an inch or so taller than Damian, and it gave him pleasure to look down at the younger man. He smiled maliciously. "Why, only that I am troubled. Do you not think it rather odd that after losing so enormous a sum, your brother has disappeared? Perhaps an accident has befallen him—or, though I would hate to think it, he has fled to the Continent. Either way, Doncaster, I hold you responsible for this debt."

Damian bent and picked up the vowel Harry had signed. It appeared to be written in his brother's hand. Had it been any other gentleman, he would have paid the note at once, although the sum was enormous. He glanced up, intending to pass off some casual remark, and caught the glint of malice in the duke's eyes. More than malice—hatred.

A sudden, unaccountable fear for Harry gripped Damian so hard that he had to swallow the bile that rose in his throat before he could speak. "This note will be redeemed, either by Harry, or by myself, within a month."

"A month? Really, Doncaster—" he began, but the look in Damian's eyes stopped him. "Oh, very well. I suppose you need time to raise the blunt, but I hope your word is better than that of your brother."

"I always keep my word," Damian said with deadly calm. "And I promise you this, *Your Grace*, if anything has happened to Harry because of you, you will not live long enough to regret it."

Cardiff shrugged. "Spare me the theatrics. I seek only payment of a debt. You have a month, no more."

Damian stepped to the bell rope and pulled it. When a liveried footman appeared a moment later, he gestured toward Cardiff. "Please show His Grace out. His business here is concluded."

After the duke left, Damian finished his brandy and set down the glass. Harry was in trouble again, that much was clear, but where in the devil was he?

"Damian?" Lady Doncaster stood in the door, her eyes troubled. "Is anything amiss?"

"Nothing for you to be concerned about," he said, managing a smile for her benefit. "But I find I shall have to go into Town on business."

She crossed to his side and laid a hand on his sleeve. "Harry is in trouble, isn't he? That odious man—oh, Damian, I am frightened."

Damn Cardiff, he thought, looking down at the only mother he had ever known. Louisa had married his father when he was four, and she had always treated him with loving kindness, if not the lavish devotion she bestowed on Harry. He hated to see her overset, but he knew it was no use attempting to deceive her.

He leaned down and kissed her brow. "Harry is in some sort of scrape, but nothing to be alarmed about. I shall find him, and send him home."

"As usual," she said, making an effort to smile even while tears brimmed her eyes.

Chapter 1

White-haired Maude Bellweather sat in her customary chair by the tall windows and watched as Miss Candace Stafford climbed into the old and weathered pony cart belonging to the vicarage. The young lady had called, as was her custom every Monday afternoon, to make certain Maude was not in need of assistance. She normally spent an hour or two at the tidy cottage, reading the paper aloud, or discussing the news of the day. This morning, however, Andrew had paid one of his rare visits and Candace, with exquisite tact, had left after only a few moments.

Andrew had walked with Miss Stafford to the door, and when he returned to the sitting room, he found his mother still staring out at the window.

"Such a pretty girl," she murmured without looking around.

"Do you think so?" he asked, wondering if his mother needed stronger spectacles. The image he retained of Miss Stafford was that of a rather plain girl. She carried herself well, but she was of unexceptional height, neither plump nor thin, though it was difficult to judge her figure beneath the ill-fitting muslin dress she had worn. Her brown hair, what he had seen of it beneath an old-fashioned

9

bonnet, had been drawn tightly back from her wide brow, and did little to flatter her. Indeed, he thought, there was nothing remarkable or distinctive about the girl, except perhaps for her green eyes, which seemed to change color according to the light.

Maude turned away from the window and glanced up at her son. He was a good boy. He provided for her generously, visited her as often as his wife would permit, and even if he lacked the perception to see what was beyond the tip of his nose, she could not complain. She smiled sweetly and inquired after her daughter-in-law.

"Elizabeth is well, and she sends her warmest regards," he said, although they both knew the sentiment was untrue. What his wife actually said was "If your mother did not insist on living in that stupid little village in the middle of nowhere, you would not need to spend an entire day calling upon her."

Uncomfortable at the lie, Andrew hastily sought to divert the conversation. He had a strong respect for his mother's powers of observation. She had been crippled by arthritis at an early age and, as a consequence, spent most of her time observing the passing world from her window. It had sharpened her perception of people, and her judgment was seldom at fault. Now he inquired curiously, "What is it about Miss Stafford you find attractive?"

Maude glanced at the window again, but Candace had disappeared. Except for the bees swarming over her rosebushes, the vista before her might have been a painting, everything was so still, like the calm before a storm. She sighed. "Candace is a natural beauty, like her mother. Do you recall a scandal about ten years ago involving Lord Blackstone?"

He thought for a moment, the name maddeningly familiar but elusive. Then it came to him and he nodded, "Yes, of course. He ran off with another man's wife, and then was killed in a duel in Paris or somewhere." Andrew had been at school, but the news of the scandal had reached even those sacred halls. For weeks it had been all anyone had talked about. But what had that to do with Miss Stafford?

As if reading his mind, his mother said softly, "Candace is the woman's daughter."

"Good Lord!"

Miss Stafford, serenely unaware that she was the topic of conversation at Mrs. Bellweather's, urged Garnet to a trot. But the afternoon sun was unusually warm, the road dusty, and the mare elderly and inclined to move at her own slow pace. Candace hesitated as she approached the lane that cut through Squire Epsom's woods.

The way looked cool and inviting, but the lane, which led from Upper Thatchwood to Lower Thatchwood, was twice as long as going around by the road. There was really no excuse for such dalliance. Indulging one's self was a sin, her uncle said. But surely, she reasoned, it could do no harm to occasionally enjoy the beauty the Lord had provided, and she was not expected back at the vicarage for an hour or two.

"Come on, Garnet," she said, pulling on the reins. The gray horse needed no further urging, and willingly drew the cart into the dappled recesses of Squire Epsom's woods. Candace allowed the mare to amble slowly along the lane while she savored the coolness the tall sycamores provided, and listened to the muted chatter of squirrels and the warbling songs of the birds. She could even hear the lazy sound of water cascading gently over rocks in the nearby stream.

Feeling unaccustomedly lethargic, Candace allowed her mind to wander . . . Jasper Fairgood, the only gentleman in Lower Thatchwood to show the slightest interest in her, had renewed his oft-repeated proposal last evening. As usual, she had put him off, but the time was coming when she must make a firm decision. She could not keep Jasper dangling forever, and yet the idea of taking vows with him, of living with him and his mother, held little appeal.

Still, she could not expect her aunt and uncle to support her indefinitely, and it was unlikely she would receive any other proposals. Jasper was a good man, she reminded herself. He was thoughtful, unfailingly kind, possessed of a tidy farm that provided him with an adequate income, and, above all, extremely respectable.

She counted off his virtues and knew she was being foolish not to accept his offer. But there was no hurry. Jasper had waited two years, and though he proposed every few months, he seemed in no more rush than she. He never demanded a firm answer, or showed any sign of impatience. Indeed, she thought, he was rather smug in his assumption that she would "come round," as he put it.

For which I should be thankful, Candace thought instead of regretting that he aroused no strong emotions in her. The one time he had tentatively dared to kiss her, she had found his embrace distasteful. But perhaps that was something a wife became accustomed to . . .

A low moan suddenly intruded on her thoughts, shattering the languor of the afternoon. The cry was so unexpected that for a moment Candace wondered if she had imagined it. She sat still, allowing Garnet to chew on a low-growing shrub, and listened intently. She heard it again, a keening cry as though some poor creature were hurt, and it seemed to come from the banks of the stream.

Candace climbed down from the cart and after tying Garnet to a tree, took the narrow footpath that sloped gently down toward the stream. The way was overgrown, obscured by the weeds growing unchecked since the squire's absence, and she trod cautiously. Even so, she nearly stumbled over the body of a young man hidden among the tall reeds that lined the banks of the stream.

Apparently, he had cried out in his sleep, but he was fully awake now. Candace stared down at him, trying to make sense of the makeshift bloody bandage tied awkwardly about his left arm, and the lethal-looking pistol clutched in his right hand.

Her gaze rose slowly, taking in the damp blond hair curled over his low brow—just the way her brother's used to do when it was wet—and a pair of light blue eyes beneath blond brows. His chin was square cut and strong, and the effect of the whole reminded her of the stubborn streak Robert got when he had been caught doing something foolish, but was determined to brave it out.

The resemblance to her brother was so strong, she admonished the young man without thinking. "Unless you intend to shoot me, I suggest you put

13

that pistol down and allow me to see what I can do to help you."

"There's nothing you can do, and if there's any sense in that pretty head of yours, you'll get back on your horse and forget you ever saw me."

She had an impression of swagger, a boyish boastfulness that would preclude his asking for help, especially from a female, though he plainly needed her assistance. Despite the gun, she did not feel afraid. Although he was older than she, there was a vulnerability in his eyes that made him seem terribly young. Or perhaps it was merely the pink Indian balsam blossoms caught on the collar of his shirt that made her think him incapable of harming her.

She took a step forward. "I cannot in good conscience do that, sir."

"I might shoot you, you know."

"Oh, do stop talking such nonsense."

He grinned at her, an engaging grin that pierced her heart with an aching loneliness for the brother she had not seen in years. It cost him, she knew, to make the effort. A second later he moaned again. The hand clutching his pistol wavered, then fell to his side as his eyes closed against an onslaught of pain. Blinking back sudden tears, she ignored his command to leave him alone and be on her way.

She knelt beside him in the damp reeds, and tenderly brushed the blond curls away from his brow. Her touch seemed to soothe him, but it frightened Candace. He was burning up with fever.

"We must get you to a doctor," she murmured, wondering if he could manage the climb to where she had left Garnet.

His blue eyes fluttered open. "No! I . . . can't risk

14

it. Just . . . go away." Then, despite his efforts, or perhaps because of them, he fainted, his head lolling back against the reeds.

Candace could not mistake the agony she had heard in his voice or the frightened way he'd looked. Gently removing the pistol from his lifeless hand, she carefully laid it aside and prepared to examine his wound. She hated to see any creature hurt, and would do whatever she could to help, but the sight of blood invariably made her nauseated. She grimaced with distaste at the sight of the bandage bound tightly around his upper arm.

It looked to be the remains of a linen handkerchief, but it was now filthy, badly stained, and impossibly knotted. Trying not to think of the rust-colored stains as blood, she worked over it until she could loosen the ends. Once she succeeded in untying the knots, Candace gently unwrapped it, exposing a jagged, gaping wound. At least it was no longer bleeding, but she detected dirt in it, and knew it would have to be cleansed.

She left him lying in the tall grass, and carefully made her way to the edge of the stream. After glancing around to make certain no one was watching, she lifted the skirt of her muslin day dress and tore the wide lace ruffle off her petticoat. Dividing it at the seam, she had two lengths of relatively clean material. One piece she dipped in the stream until it was sopping, then carefully carried both back to where she'd left the young man.

It did not appear that he had moved. She knelt again, cradling his blond head in her lap, and gently cleansed the wound. While she was not knowledgeable about gunshot injuries, she had seen them on two occasions when her uncle had called on her to assist him. This looked very similar, and fortunately it appeared the bullet had only creased his arm rather than entered it.

When all traces of dirt and dried blood had been removed, she used the other length to bind his arm tightly. As she was tying the bandage securely, she became aware that he was watching her.

"How long have you been awake?" she asked, suddenly aware of the impropriety of sitting with his head in her lap.

"Not long," he muttered. "I thought . . . you'd left."

She ignored that. "This wound requires a doctor's attention. If you—" She broke off as he struggled to sit up and turned to face her.

"No doctor," he growled. "And I must ask you not to mention my presence here to anyone."

"Are you in trouble with the law? Is that why you are afraid to seek help?"

He shook his head, the blond curls falling over his brow, and again she was reminded of her brother.

"I give you my word, I have done nothing wrong, but someone took a shot at me . . . it was deliberate."

Candace studied him for a moment. His voice was educated, his white frilled shirt, though dirty and tattered, was well tailored and of the finest lawn, and his tight-fitting yellow pantaloons were of excellent cut. On his right hand he wore a large square-cut emerald set in a wide gold band. All indications of a young man from a good family, possibly a member of the aristocracy.

"Well?" he demanded. "Do I pass muster?"

"I beg your pardon?"

16

"Do I meet with your approval?" he asked, giving her a crooked grin. "You were staring, Miss—?"

"Stafford," she replied absently.

"You will forgive me for not rising, I hope, but I am pleased to make your acquaintance. Harry Reynald at your service, Miss Stafford. And thank you, for this," he said, indicating the bandage on his arm.

"Do not thank me," she said, rising to her feet. "That arm needs a doctor's attention, and I am certain you have a fever."

"Probably. I have been out here all night, and I haven't eaten since yesterday. I say, you don't happen to have a bit of food stashed anywhere? A crust of bread?"

Candace shook her head. "I am sorry, but if you will come with me, we can see that your arm is tended and provide you with a decent meal. My uncle—"

"I appreciate your offer, Miss Stafford," he interrupted, "but I don't want *anyone* to know where I am until I figure out who in the devil tried to shoot me, and why."

"Perhaps it was an accident," she suggested. "A poacher or hunter."

"This happened just north of London—and whoever did it has been trying to finish the job ever since. Someone tried again last night, which is when I hightailed it into the woods here."

"Oh. But I cannot just leave you."

"If you really wish to help, say nothing to anyone, and bring me back something to eat."

There was no point in arguing with him. He looked every bit as obstinate as Robert when he got the bit between his teeth. She hesitated, then sug-

17

gested, "There is a deserted gamekeeper's hut not far from here. Perhaps you could sleep there—at least for tonight. Then tomorrow I could bring you some food."

"Not till tomorrow? Never mind—how far is this hut?"

"Just up the hill, and through the woods a little way. I think if you lean on me, you should be able to make the climb."

Harry reluctantly agreed, and allowed Candace to help him up. After stowing his pistol in his waistband, he placed his right arm around her shoulders, and they started awkwardly up the bank. Progress was slow. Harry had to stop to rest every few feet, and Candace feared he would pass out again before she got him to the cottage.

It took nearly an hour, but at last they came to the small glade where the deserted hut stood, its door hanging crookedly ajar. He nodded approvingly and then leaned against the hut while Candace pulled the door open.

The interior was dark and dusty, and it was plain no one had been inside the place in some considerable time. The cottage consisted of one large room, dominated by an old stone fireplace in the center. To the left of the door was a narrow cot covered by a tattered patchwork quilt. On the right, a roughly made table and two chairs formed a tiny dining area. Beside the table, a rusted bucket stood on the floor.

Candace hurried across the room and pulled the curtains open on the two small windows so the afternoon light filtered in. If possible, the hut looked worse.

Harry stepped in and surveyed the room. "Not

the best accommodations I've had, but better than
... some."

Candace crossed quickly to his side and helped
him to the cot. "You are exhausted. Lie here and
rest. I will get you some water before I leave, and
I believe there may be some berries growing
nearby."

"Just ... just the water, please," he muttered. "I
shall probably sleep till morning."

Chapter 2

The sleepy inhabitants of Upper Thatchwood were just beginning to stir early on Tuesday morning when the Earl of Doncaster guided his team of chestnuts into the quiet courtyard of the village's only inn. The sun, just cresting over the tops of the trees, pushed through a bank of storm clouds and glinted off a garishly painted sign that proclaimed the establishment to be the Boar's Head Inn. Only a dilapidated pony cart, harnessed to a tired-looking gray mare, stood in the yard. Small, with no hostlers in sight, the inn was not the sort of place Damian normally patronized. But then, nothing about the past two days bore the slightest resemblance to normalcy. He sighed as he expertly drew his team to a standstill. Both he and his groom desperately needed rest.

He turned to suggest Paddy wait in the carriage, but the words died on his lips. Amazing, he thought, the way the tiny Irishman could drop off to sleep while traveling across some of the worst roads in England. Slumped against the carriage seat with his chin resting on his chest, and wisps of unruly red hair standing on end, Paddy looked more than ever like the bantam rooster Damian dubbed him.

"Don't allow me to disturb you," the earl murmured sarcastically, but he retrieved Paddy's hat from the floorboard and placed it gently on his groom's head to shade his eyes against the emerging sun. Perhaps it was just as well Paddy slept, he thought. While there was no better man to have at one's back in a fight, his groom tended to speak his mind. Discretion was not in his vocabulary. And at the moment they needed to be discreet.

The earl climbed down from his curricle and tied the reins to the hitching post. He stretched, then brushed futilely at the dust covering his pantaloons before crossing the yard. He would inquire for his brother here, but if there was no news of Harry, he would still book a room. After driving through the past two nights, he was tired, dirty, and frustrated.

Damian stepped into the inn's parlor, a tiny room crammed with an ill assortment of mismatched furniture. The only occupant was a dab of a girl who stood near a makeshift desk that blocked the entrance to the rear rooms. Damian barely noticed her. He strode directly to the desk and called out for the innkeeper.

Candace Stafford eyed the tall stranger curiously from beneath the wide brim of her straw hat. Though his clothes were creased and dirty, the authoritative ring in his voice bespoke of Quality. She quickly turned away as the gentleman looked in her direction.

"Is there no one in this place?" he demanded.

"Any number of people, but if you are seeking a room, Mrs. Marley should be out in a moment," she replied, her voice a gentle rebuke. Although it was an unchristian thing to do, she then deliberately turned her shoulder to him. The man had the sort of arrogance she associated with the nobility. She despised so-called gentlemen who behaved as though no one had anything better to do than instantly see to their comfort.

Damian, tired as he was, heard the thinly disguised contempt in the woman's voice. When she pointedly turned her back to him, his dark eyes crinkled with amusement and his heavy black brows rose in surprise. He knew he was no hand with the ladies—not like his younger brother—but females seldom treated him with such marked scorn.

His attention was distracted by the appearance of an older, heavyset woman waddling through the door. Busy wiping her hands on her flour-covered apron, she didn't look up as she spoke.

"Your basket will be ready in a trice, Miss Stafford, as soon as that good-for-nothing Daisy puts up the sandwiches—" She broke off her words abruptly when she saw Damian standing near the desk. "Good heavens, why didn't someone tell me we have a guest? Morning, sir. Would you be wanting a room?"

"Possibly," Damian said. "But please finish your business with Miss Stafford. I can wait."

"Oh, she's all done, sir. Just waiting on her pick-a-nick basket," Mrs. Marley declared, emphasizing the words in a high singsong voice. She leaned across the desk and confided, "Though I told her, it looks like rain coming on. Not the best sort of weather for a pick-a-nick, but you know how these young folks are. Get a notion into their heads, and there's no persuading them otherwise. No sense at all until they get to be our age."

"Indeed," Damian agreed politely, while wondering if his eight-and-twenty years were really sufficient to classify him as a contemporary of the innkeeper. Apparently it was, in Mrs. Marley's mind. He tried the effect of a smile, leaned against the desk, and confided, "As it happens, I am seeking just such a young person. He is of my height, but blond and blue-eyed and quite foolish enough to go on a picnic when the clouds are building. His name is Harry Reynald."

Miss Stafford gasped and spun around. For an instant her green eyes regarded him with alarm. Then thick lashes swept down to hide her emotions.

"I . . . I am sorry. I did not mean to interrupt," she murmured when he glanced in her direction. "A pin pricked my finger." She quickly turned away and pretended an inordinate interest in the view outside the window.

Damian had stopped at the Boar's Head Inn more for rest than in expectation of hearing any news of Harry. But the girl's reaction was interesting, perhaps worth pursuing. He eyed her speculatively before returning his attention to the innkeeper.

Mrs. Marley shoved an escaping strand of graying hair back into her untidy bun, and looked at Damian regretfully. "Can't say as I've seen such a one about, but if he's anywhere near, sir, this is where he'd come. The Boar's Head is the only inn this side of the river."

"I see. Well, if you should happen to meet him, I would take it kindly if you would let him know that . . . Edward Croyden is looking for him," Damian said, hesitating over revealing his true identity.

He had learned enough in the past week to know that Harry was in serious trouble. But from whom, or why, Damian was not sure. He suspected the Duke of Cardiff might be involved, but if His Grace merely wanted payment of his note, it didn't make sense to send a couple of thugs after Harry. And someone was definitely chasing his brother.

Until he knew more, Damian thought it safer to travel as plain Edward Croyden, using his two middle names. Harry would understand at once if he could get a message to him, but, hopefully, no one else would.

Mrs. Marley frowned, disappointment showing in the sagging muscles of her double chins. "You'll not be wanting a room, then?"

"On the contrary. My groom and I have been traveling all night. If you can accommodate us, I would like two rooms."

The landlady, her smile instantly restored, assured him, "We'd be pleased to have you. I'll just send one of my boys out for your baggage—"

Damian shook his head, interrupting her. "Pray, do not trouble yourself. I haven't much, and there are one or two matters I must attend to first. If you could just see that the rooms are ready in an hour?" At Mrs. Marley's nod, he moved toward the door, sparing one last look for the young lady who remained obstinately by the windows.

Candace Stafford breathed a sigh of relief as Mr. Croyden left the inn. She had nearly given herself away when he'd mentioned he was looking for Mr. Reynald, for she had been thinking of Harry at precisely that moment. Hearing his name suddenly spoken aloud had startled her. She remembered his warning that someone was following him, someone who wished him dead.

Despite his wound, she had not entirely believed Harry Reynald's tale, and set much of his fear down to dramatics. He reminded her of her cousins, both of whom were given to embroidering the truth to make it a bit more exciting. But now, with the presence of this ominous-looking stranger asking questions about him, she began to think Harry had been speaking the truth.

Fidgeting impatiently, Candace waited for her basket. Yesterday, she had thought Harry foolish for not seeking help, but even so she could not let him starve. Knowing it would be impossible to spirit any amount of food out of the vicarage without her aunt noticing, Candace had used the last of her allowance to order Harry a sufficient supply of food from the inn, and she'd planned to deliver it that morning. She had viewed it as a simple act of Christian charity. But now she felt a new sense of urgency, and wished Mrs. Marley would hurry. She must warn Harry immediately that Edward Croyden was searching for him.

"Here's your basket, Miss Stafford," Mrs. Marley said, lifting a heavy wicker case over the desk. Curiosity lit her eyes. "Gracious, there's enough food in there to feed a dozen young people. Must be quite a pick-a-nick you're planning."

"Thank you," Candace replied sweetly as she paid for the basket while ignoring the woman's broad hints.

"I sure hope you and your friends don't get rained on. Mr. Marley says a storm's blowing up. His knee's aching something fierce, and that's a sure sign."

"I shall keep that in mind," Candace promised, edging toward the door. It opened before she reached it, admitting two large, heavyset men. The taller one in the drab gray driving coat looked her up and down insolently. Blushing, she quickly stepped outside, but her relief was short-lived.

Edward Croyden sat in his carriage, next to her pony cart, his gaze intent on the door. She clenched her hands to control their trembling, but she could not still the rapid beating of her heart. She knew with a certainty that he had deliberately waited for her.

Doing her best to ignore his probing stare, and that of the disreputable-looking fellow seated beside him, Candace walked stiffly to her cart and stowed the basket. She fumbled with the reins as she untied them, uncomfortably aware that the two men watched her every movement.

Pretend you do not see them, she told herself, but found it difficult to do. And, naturally, Garnet chose that moment to behave mulishly. Candace jerked on the reins until the elderly mare finally responded by lifting her head and glancing around. She surveyed her mistress with baleful eyes.

"Come on, Garnet," Candace pleaded. "You *cannot* go to sleep now. Be a good girl, and I will see you get an extra helping of oats when we get home."

Betwixt her coaxing and judicious use of the reins, Candace got the mare moving out of the yard, and at a reasonable trot down the center of High Street. For Garnet, it was high speed. Candace relaxed slightly, her mind intent on Harry.

Lost in thought, it was several moments before she heard the sound of a carriage coming up behind her. She glanced over her shoulder, alarmed to see Edward Croyden following her. He waved, a jaunty salute that did little to instill her with confidence.

Unnerved, she drove on for a quarter mile. The relentless roll of the carriage wheels and steady pounding of hoofbeats behind her seemed to grow louder and louder. Finding it difficult to think clearly, Candace ordered herself to remain calm. Edward Croyden could have no reason to follow her unless . . . unless he was after Harry Reynald. Horrified, she realized she must have given herself away at the inn, and Mr. Croyden suspected she had some knowledge of Harry. The idea took hold, and in another moment she had convinced herself it was the only possible explanation.

She glanced back again. Was it only her imagination, or was his carriage drawing closer? Knowing it was hopeless to expect Garnet to move any faster, she pulled slightly to the side of the road. She prayed Croyden would give her the go-by. But he stayed just behind her, the assiduous sound of his carriage wheels grating on her nerves.

She thought of Harry, lying helpless, unable to defend himself, in the gamekeeper's hut. She could not lead this stranger to him.

The only thing to do was confront Mr. Croyden.

Abruptly, Candace guided the mare off the road and waited. When the dusty black curricle pulled to a halt alongside her own cart, she demanded, "Why are you following me, sir?"

"Following you?" Damian asked with feigned surprise. "Why, I believe you flatter yourself, Miss Stafford. Perhaps you have never noticed that High Street is the only road out of the village?"

Now that he could see her more clearly, Damian realized the lady was younger than he'd supposed—about eighteen, he estimated. And prettier, too, or she would be if she didn't dress so plainly. His gaze raked over her, and he added, "You really should not be driving alone. Some unscrupulous fellow might accost you."

Candace glanced behind her, wishing someone, anyone, would come along. She would even welcome the sight of Jasper Fairgood, if he would only rescue her from Mr. Croyden's smoky, knowing gaze.

Swallowing hard, she turned to face him again and tried to speak with cool unconcern. "What I do is none of your affair, sir. Please be so good as to drive on."

Surprised and irritated by her imperious tone, Damian tossed the reins to Paddy and climbed down from his curricle. Between the merry chase his brother had led him, and now this chit of a girl ordering him about, he was at the end of his patience. He crossed swiftly to the pony cart. Before the young lady realized what he was about, he had hoisted himself up on the seat and sat glowering at her. "I will gladly be on my way, Miss Stafford— just as soon as you answer a few questions."

Candace looked up at him. Although he was not as old as she had first thought, he seemed much more menacing when viewed so closely. She noted the broad shoulders beneath his smooth-fitting coat, the dark growth of beard on a strong chin that had not been shaved in several days, and the large hand placed above hers on the reins. His tightly gloved fingers were slender, but his hand measured twice the size of her own and she could easily imagine it around her throat if she dared to gainsay him.

Brutish lout. Her back stiffened and she braced her shoulders as though fearing a blow, but bravely kept her eyes fixed on his. "If you were any sort of gentleman, you would leave this carriage at once."

"And if you were any sort of lady, you would not be on the road alone. Why, any man might be tempted to stop you and steal a kiss ..." He leaned suggestively toward her, shifting his weight slightly.

Candace drew back, prepared to leap down from the cart if necessary.

"Fortunately for you, Miss Stafford, I want only information about Harry Reynald," Damian continued smoothly. "You heard me ask Mrs. Marley about him, and you recognized the description. You have seen him, have you not? Tell me where I can find him—it is of the utmost importance."

"I cannot help you, sir," she replied, averting her gaze. Staring straight ahead, she added with chilling politeness, "Now, would you please be good enough to remove yourself from my carriage? My family is expecting me at home and will become concerned do I not arrive soon."

"Indeed? I thought you were going on a picnic—is that not what the proprietress at the inn said?"

"Mrs. Marley was mistaken," Candace declared, a blush creeping up her neck at the outright lie. She edged away from Croyden, but his hand clamped over her arm.

"Then where are you going, Miss Stafford?"

Candace glanced down at the gloved fingers resting against the olive green of her dress, and then up at Croyden. She knew she was no match for his strength, but she hated men who bullied women,

29

and her anger fueled her courage. She glared at him and said coldly, "If you will not remove yourself, then you leave me little choice but to walk."

Damian sighed. He knew she was lying about Harry, and he'd like to throttle the truth out of her, but he was no better at intimidating ladies than he was at courting them. He released his hold on her arm, and sat idly watching her for a moment. She refused to meet his gaze. "I shall leave you for now, Miss Stafford, but I promise we shall meet again."

"Not if I can avoid it," she said defiantly as he started to climb down from the cart. She snapped the reins. For once, Garnet obeyed promptly. As the cart jerked forward, Edward Croyden tumbled to the road. She glanced back and saw him sitting ignobly in the dirt.

Cursing beneath his breath, the earl watched her drive off, then rose and returned wearily to his own carriage. Paddy sat on the seat, a wide grin on his leprechaun face.

"So much as a word out of you, and I will sack you," Damian warned.

Unconcerned, the groom laughed aloud. "Save your threats for the young lady, my lord. *She* might be afraid of you, the way you threatened her and all."

"I did not threaten her," Damian insisted, taking the reins. He turned the carriage and headed back to the inn. "I was merely trying to get the truth out of the girl. She knows something about Harry—I would stake my life on that."

Paddy sobered abruptly. Like most of the staff at Deerpark, he was devoted to Damian and Harry. No one could ask for a better or fairer man to work for than the earl, and being around the young master was like basking in the light of the sun. He had a warm smile and a cheerful word for everyone. Problem was, Harry never set his mind to anything but having fun. He was off on one lark after another—with his lordship having to bail him out of trouble more often than not.

At first Paddy had thought Harry's disappearance was just another of his mad capers, but after the last two nights, he, too, was worried. Three times they'd crossed the trail of two other men seeking news of Harry, men that Paddy didn't like the sound of. He felt in his bones they were the reason Harry had gone to ground.

Damian kept his own counsel, merely saying that it was not like his brother to avoid a fight. Which was true enough, but even a blind man could see Harry was hiding from someone. Paddy sighed, recalling the last few days. They'd tracked the boy out of London, and he'd avoided towns of any size, staying instead in out-of-the-way villages and inns he'd normally not touch. And he'd needed money.

His lordship had found his brother's carriage, sold for a pittance in a place called Swineshead. Paddy scowled at the thought of that beautiful, custom-made carriage going for a tenth of its value to a farmer who would not appreciate it. For sure, Harry was in trouble. Damian thought he was making for Greenbriar—the small estate near York that Harry's grandfather had left him, but if he was, the lad was taking the long way around.

And now they'd lost track of him.

"He is here somewhere, Paddy. I am sure of it," Damian said. "We'll put up at the inn and get some sleep. Then you nose about and see what you can discover."

31

Paddy agreed. Sleep sounded grand. He had nothing but catnaps for two days and felt so tired that if he stumbled over Harry's horse, he would not recognize it. And his lordship wasn't in much better shape. He cast an eye at Damian. "You'll be getting a bit of rest, too, my lord?"

The earl nodded. "Aye. Then I shall see what I can learn about Miss Stafford."

"She didn't seem the type to be carrying on with Master Harry."

"Perhaps not, but I'm certain she recognized his name. And she told the innkeeper that she was going on a picnic—which she clearly was not dressed for—and on a day when it is bound to rain." Damian glanced up at the ominous storm clouds. He could feel the dampness in the air.

"I don't see what difference it makes whether she picnics or not," Paddy groused, thinking only of the inn and bed.

"Perhaps none, but all the same I would very much like to know where she was headed with that basket of food. And I intend to find out."

Chapter 3

After looking behind her for the fourth time to make certain that Mr. Croyden was no longer following her, Candace turned off High Street. She carefully maneuvered her cart onto the rough lane leading to Squire Epsom's. He had not been in residence for several years, and the way was choked with weeds to the point where it was nearly impassable. Fortunately, she did not have far to go. She reined in Garnet and sat still.

It appeared Mrs. Marley was right about the storm, Candace thought, hoping the rain would hold off until she had seen Harry. Feeling a trifle chilly, she pulled her cape closer about her. Deep woods lined both sides of the road, the tall sycamores casting their shadows across it. Leaves rustled as the wind picked up strength and swept through the trees, but she heard no ominous sound. No hoofbeats. No carriage wheels. Only the clear, sweet notes of a willow warbler and the mingled cries of blackbirds and magpies broke the silence.

She waited a quarter-hour, alert for any sign that she might have been followed, but the only creature moving in the area was a small brown rabbit. She watched it dart across the drive in front of her cart.

A red squirrel, gaining courage, chattered at her from the safety of his branch.

When she was certain Mr. Croyden was no longer following her, she tied Garnet to a shrub and lifted down the heavy wicker case. It was awkward to carry so far, but the footpath leading to the hut was not wide enough for the cart, and she had not dared to come on horseback.

Today was Tuesday, and on Tuesday mornings Candace routinely took the pony cart and paid visits to the sick. It was expected of her. Had she deviated this morning, Uncle Jonathan would have questioned her. She hated deceiving him, but she could not tell him the truth. She had wrestled with the problem for most of the night, knowing that a lie by omission was just as sinful as an outright lie. But even if Harry hadn't sworn her to secrecy, her uncle would have been deeply concerned that she had been alone in the woods with a young man—especially a young man of noble birth. She had guessed, from things Harry had said and from his manner, that he came from an aristocratic family, a mark against him in her uncle's judgment book.

She left the drive and started the trek up the footpath, thinking about her uncle. She was only eight years old when her father had brought her to live at the vicarage with his brother and wife, but even then Uncle Jonathan had warned her she must be on guard against her frivolous nature. For years Candace had not understood what he meant, and Aunt Emily would never answer her questions.

And she'd had lots of questions. There was something odd about the way her mother had disappeared just before she died, but it made Aunt Emily uneasy to talk about it. Gradually, Candace had quit asking, and quit longing for her father to come see her. Or Robert. Her brother used to visit her every few months, but she had not seen him since he'd enlisted in the army two years earlier. He was somewhere on the Peninsula now—at least he had been when he last wrote.

She missed Robert. Although her aunt and uncle treated her with loving kindness, and her cousins were like sisters, she still longed for her own family. Candace knew it was foolish of her, but sometimes she felt as though everyone were just waiting for her to put a foot wrong, to behave like her mother. It was nonsense, of course, but she could never quite forget that day when she was fifteen.

The day she had learned the truth about her mother.

Thomasina, a year older than Candace, walked out that spring with her first beau. Aunt Emily had been in a tizzy of excitement, and Theresa, a year younger, near green with envy. Candace wondered at all the fuss. It was only Cyril Bakersfield, a gangly lad with a pockmarked face, though he was the elder son of Sir Bonamy.

In the way that sisters do at that age, she'd bickered with Thomasina over him, taunting her cousin about her unhandsome beau. She had made the mistake of telling Thomasina she wouldn't want to marry such a one, baronet's son or not.

"You'll be lucky if a man like Cyril looks at you, much less deigns to marry you," her cousin retorted.

"Why wouldn't he?" Candace asked innocently. She might not be as pretty as her blond cousin, but there was nothing about her to repulse a gentleman.

"Because of the scandal," Theresa blurted out, then covered her mouth with her hand.

"Idiot," Thomasina scolded. "Can you not keep your wretched mouth shut about anything?"

"What scandal?" Candace demanded. The sick look on her younger cousin's face was enough to make her own stomach turn uncomfortably.

"Please don't ask me," Theresa begged. "Papa will be so angry if I tell you. He made us swear never to say a word."

Not entirely sure she wanted to know, but driven by a need she didn't understand, Candace pressed her. "You might as well tell me what you are talking about, or I shall go down and ask Uncle Jonathan myself."

Her two cousins eyed each other for a moment, then Thomasina crossed the small room to sit on the bed beside Candace. "I shall tell you what I know, but you must swear never to mention it to Papa. We have been forbidden to speak of the matter, and you know what Papa is like if his wishes are not obeyed."

Candace agreed, crossing her heart and swearing an oath of secrecy.

"We only found out when Robert came to see you that last time. He was talking to Mama in the kitchen and did not realize we were in the pantry. They were discussing your mother, and how much you look like her."

Candace nodded. Her uncle had remarked the resemblance several times.

"Mama said . . . she said she hoped you would not turn out like Aunt Diana, that it was a terrible thing she did. We thought she had just died, you know, but when Mama realized we heard her, she told us the truth." Thomasina swallowed hard, then continued. "Aunt Diana ran off with a marquis! She left your papa, and your brother, and you, and fled to Paris with this Lord Blackstone. Mama said Aunt Diana was in love with him and could not help herself, but Papa said she had been tempted by the devil and we must pray for her."

Candace closed her eyes, the color draining from her face. She remembered her mama as an angel, with a cloud of dark hair and green eyes much like her own, a slender creature who always smelled heavenly and whose smile lit the room.

"Candace? I *am* sorry," Thomasina said, reaching for her cousin's hand. "Mama told me Uncle Charles could not bear to have you near him because you reminded him so much of Aunt Diana. That is why he brought you here to live."

A number of things suddenly made sense to Candace. She opened her eyes, willing herself not to cry in front of her cousins. "And Mama? Is it true that she died, or is she still in Paris with . . . him?"

Thomasina nodded sadly. "That much is true. She . . . she died a few months later. They say Lord Blackstone fought a duel with a gentleman who dared to insult her. He was killed, and Aunt Diana was so grief-stricken, she . . . she took his pistol and shot herself. Oh, Candace, say something. I feel absolutely dreadful, and I wish Theresa had never said a word."

"You started it," her sister muttered.

"It does not matter," Candace said, rising. She forced a smile to her lips. "I am glad you told me the truth, and I promise to say nothing to Uncle Jonathan. Now, if you will leave me, I should like to be alone for a while."

37

That was the first evening Candace had coiled her long brown hair into a tight bun at the back of her neck. It was not a becoming style, but Uncle Jonathan had instantly approved. And Candace had worn it in the same manner ever since.

She set out to prove she was nothing like her mother. Unlike Theresa and Thomasina, who flouted their papa's rules whenever he was absent, Candace obeyed him strictly. She never joined her cousins in idle gossip or flirted with any of the young men in the village. She was the one who wrote out her uncle's sermons for him when he complained his wife's handwriting was nearly illegible. And Candace had gradually assumed the responsibility of visiting the sick for Aunt Emily, who complained that being among the ill made her distinctly queasy.

From that day until the moment she had stumbled across Harry Reynald, Candace had never given her uncle the slightest cause for concern. Indeed, he often said she was a model of decorum whose example his daughters would do well to follow.

He would not think so were he to see her this morning, Candace thought ruefully as she neared the gamekeeper's cottage. But she could not leave Harry to fend for himself. Not when he reminded her so much of Robert, and not when he so desperately needed her help.

She approached the hut warily. It was situated in a small clearing, now overgrown with Indian balsam. The tall, pink-flowering plants almost obscured it from view. Only someone who knew its precise location could find it from the bridle path—

which was one of the reasons she had chosen to hide Harry in the deserted cottage.

Shifting the weight of the hamper, she circled to the front of the building and tapped lightly on the door. Harry didn't answer, but she thought he might be sleeping and quietly pushed the door open. One glance was sufficient to see that the place was empty.

The sound of a footstep behind her scared Candace. She dropped the basket and whirled around.

Harry stood just outside the door, his pistol raised in his right hand.

Exasperated, her heart still hammering from fright, Candace glared at him. "It is extremely impolite of you, Mr. Reynald, to continue waving that pistol at me every time I come to assist you. Pray, put it down before you accidentally set it off."

Harry lowered the pistol and grinned at her. It was his smile, she decided, that reminded her so much of Robert.

"I apologize, Miss Stafford, but you need not worry—I am an excellent shot."

"Pardon me for contradicting you, sir, but if you are as good as you claim, how is it that you have a bullet in your shoulder?"

"The other fellow did not play fair—he shot from the trees, which is why I am a trifle edgy. I say, I hope that basket contains food. I am famished." He stowed his pistol and limped into the cottage.

"What is wrong with your leg?" Candace asked, noticing his lameness at once. Yesterday, he had complained only of his arm.

Harry reddened. "I tripped over an uprooted willow tree when I walked out to look for you. 'Tis nothing." But it was obvious the leg pained him when he lowered himself to one of the chairs by the table.

"I hope you did not have your pistol at the ready when you fell. You could have been seriously injured." Nettled by his superior manner, she added, "Perhaps that is what really happened to your arm."

Insulted, he frowned up at her and started to rise. "I told you, Miss Stafford, I was shot at by someone in the woods. As far as I know, the same person is still after me. If you do not believe me—"

"Oh, sit down. As it happens, I do believe you," she interrupted. Then, bending over to the basket, she removed a linen cloth, spread it over the dusty table, and lifted out a loaf of fresh-baked bread, which Harry reached for at once. "There is ham, and some excellent cheese to go with that, or cold chicken if you prefer it," she remarked.

He nodded, his mouth full.

Candace hesitated. She didn't want to alarm him, but he needed to know about Edward Croyden. She waited until he had taken another bite, then explained, "I had the basket packed at an inn in Upper Thatchwood, and while I was waiting for it, a gentleman came in inquiring for you."

Harry swallowed hastily, all attention now. "What did he look like?"

"Dangerous," she said, remembering a pair of dark, smoky eyes.

"Can you not do better than that?" He bit off another chunk of bread and questioned her with his mouth full. "Was he tall? Short? Fat or lean?"

"Rather tall, and broad-shouldered. He had wavy,

black hair, thick, shaggy brows, and, I suspect, a violent temper. He said his name is Edward Croyden."

Harry choked on the bread and suffered a violent fit of coughing.

Candace quickly opened the wine and poured him a portion in the pewter cup she'd packed. She passed it to him with an admonishment not to eat so quickly.

Harry drained the cup, and handed it back to her with a gesture to fill it again. The description sounded amazingly like his brother, except for the part about him looking dangerous and having a violent temper. Damian was a large man, and with his dark hair and brows, one might, he supposed, take him to be formidable at first glance, but his brother had the patience of a saint, as Harry well knew.

His own mother frequently remarked that if only her son had Damian's exquisite manners, her every wish would be fulfilled. Damian, she said, was so thoughtful, so considerate, so conscious in every way of the obligation due his family . . . the list went on and on until Harry was driven to do something outrageous.

"Do you know Mr. Croyden?" Candace asked, intruding on his thoughts.

"Possibly," Harry hedged. "Though if he's the fellow I believe he is, I cannot imagine what he would be doing in—gads, I do not even know where I am. What's the name of this village?"

"Lower Thatchwood," she replied with a smile.

"Never heard of the place."

"The stream I found you by flows into Hebden Water, and Gibson Mill is not far from here. Have you heard of it? I believe it to be fairly well known for its textile manufacturing."

Harry shook his head. "Can't say as I have ever heard of it, and I doubt my—er—Mr. Croyden knows of it either. The last I heard he was . . . uh . . . managing his estate, which is situated a good ways south of here."

"An estate? Well, I suppose he could be a landed gentleman—he had the arrogance for it," she said, remembering the rude way he'd treated her. Fairness compelled her to add, "His carriage was unexceptional, though I did admire his horses—a showy pair of chestnuts. Still, he was traveling with only a gnome of a man whose demeanor was hardly that of a proper servant."

Paddy. That cinched it, Harry thought, but how on earth had Damian tracked him here, and why had he bothered? And why was he masquerading as plain Mr. Croyden and traveling with only his groom instead of his usual entourage?

Harry reached absently for a piece of chicken, thinking of his half brother. They had not parted on the best of terms. Harry had lost a foolish wager that resulted in his accidentally setting a neighbor's barn on fire—a mishap that could have befallen anyone. Damian had lectured him severely, which was not all that unusual, but this time he had refused to pay for the damages.

Appealing to his mother had been useless. Harry had seen the look of disappointment in her eyes, and had not needed to hear her words spoken aloud to know that she wished, yet once again, that he were more like Damian. Stung, Harry had left the following morning, determined to show them both that he was as good a man as his brother. And he would have if his plans had not suddenly gone awry in London. Nothing he couldn't handle, of course, though being shot at was an unnerving experience. Still, after that last lecture, he would rot in this bloody hut before asking Damian for help.

"What should I tell him?"

"I beg your pardon?" Harry said, abruptly recalled to attention.

"I said, what do you wish me to tell Mr. Croyden? He is putting up at the inn in Upper Thatchwood, and it is possible I may encounter him again." Candace shuddered slightly, remembering Croyden's parting words. If he had his way, she would definitely meet him again.

"Why, you must deny all knowledge of me," Harry answered with a lazy smile. "It would do your reputation no good if it became known you had a tryst in the gamekeeper's cottage with a strange gentleman."

"My reputation is not the point, Mr. Reynald, and if you had listened to me yesterday, and allowed me to take you to Dr. Forbes, it would not be necessary for me to ... to tryst—"

Harry hooted with laughter. "Believe me, Miss Stafford, this is not my notion of a tryst. I was only teasing you."

"Then please cease doing so at once," she said, a blush coloring her cheeks. The truth was her reputation would suffer greatly. This was exactly the sort of situation her uncle had tried to guard her from, and it would not matter in the least that she was not at all attracted to Harry Reynald. She stood, picking up the basket, which she must return before Aunt Emily noticed it was gone.

"Forgive me, Miss Stafford," Harry said, rising

awkwardly to his feet. "I am greatly indebted to you for assisting me when it would have been much easier for you to have left me down there by the stream."

She was about to reply when he clutched at his heart, his voice rising dramatically. "Of course, had you not intervened, I would have likely starved to death . . ."

"Are you never serious, sir?"

"Rarely. Are you always so somber?"

Candace sighed. "Pray sit down and allow me to examine your arm before I leave. I brought some basilicum powder, which should help guard against infection, and some clean bandages, but I have not much time to spare."

"Where are you off to in such a hurry?" Harry teased. "I suppose there is a young man waiting for you?"

"Hardly. I am expected back at the vicarage. Indeed, I should have returned home by now."

"Oh, Lord, never tell me you are a parson's daughter!"

"No," Candace said as she gently unwound her makeshift bandage, "merely the vicar's niece."

"Well, I suppose that explains why you're so . . ." He hesitated, allowing his words to trail off.

"Somber?" she suggested, but this time a smile curved her lips.

"Efficient," Harry amended, grinning up at her. "When you smile like that, Miss Stafford, you do not look in the least somber. But, I say, I am sorry for embroiling you in my affairs. If I had known—"

"Hush. Helping the sick and the dying are part of my duties."

44

"I hope I don't fall in the latter category," he murmured, wincing slightly as she cleansed his wound.

"Not yet," she replied. She had meant only to tease, but she shivered suddenly with a premonition of trouble to come.

Damian, feeling considerably better after sleeping deeply for several hours, completed his transformation with a bath, shave, and change of raiment. Unfortunately, there was little he could do about his boots. He momentarily regretted not bringing along Phipps, who had the dressing of him, and a way of blacking the Hessians that made Damian the envy of many gentlemen.

But Phipps would have deplored his master's current mode of travel, and no doubt resigned his post half a dozen times. Damian eyed his boots. Surely, it could not be so difficult to achieve a credible shine. He wiped the accumulated dust off as best he could with a damp cloth, then poured a few drops of ale on a clean linen handkerchief. The result would have brought tears to Phipps's eyes had he been present, but Damian deemed his efforts adequate.

He shrugged into his coat, thankful he'd resisted his valet's efforts to have his clothes tailored so tightly that one required assistance to put them on. The jacket fit comfortably across his shoulders, and he need have no fear of bursting a seam if he so much as flexed his arms.

Satisfied, Damian started for the door but halted as a light tap sounded. Every sense alert for trouble, he waited.

"Governor? You in there, gov?"

"Come in, Paddy," Damian said as he swung open

the door. "And try not to let everyone in the place know we're here."

"Ain't no one about to hear me," Paddy replied indignantly. "Why, we got more people mucking out the stables at home than what lives in this village."

"Excellent."

Paddy gaped at his master, wondering if the earl had taken leave of his senses. His lordship *looked* well enough, but he was unconcernedly adjusting the ruffles at his wrists, just as though he'd not a care in the world.

"Close your mouth, Paddy," Damian suggested gently. "It occurs to me that the less people about, the easier it will be to hear any news of Harry."

"Humph—if he's here."

"He's here, I am certain of it, and that young lady we encountered this morning knows where he is hiding. I intend to better my acquaintance with Miss Stafford. Now, did you get any sleep?"

The groom grinned, a gap-toothed smile that produced a dozen new wrinkles in his weathered face. "Slept like the dead. You coulda picked me up and dropped me in the river without me turning a hair."

"Then I suggest you take one of the horses and search the area. Harry might be easy to hide, but if he's still riding that black stallion of his—and I cannot image him parting with Majestic for any reason—you might spot it."

Paddy nodded. He wasn't entirely convinced, but he knew his employer to be a shrewd one. If the earl believed his half brother was hiding somewhere hereabouts, like as not it was true. No one knew Harry better.

Damian, praying he was right in his deductions, took a pinch of snuff after his groom left, then strolled down to the taproom. It was deserted, save for the proprietor, Phineas T. Marley.

An enormous man, he moved lightly on his feet. As Damian settled at a table, he was there to wipe if off. Of course, the rag he used was filthy, but the earl tried not to notice and answered the innkeeper's greeting warmly.

"What can I be getting you? A bit of ale to quench your thirst?"

Damian nodded and removed a few pound notes from his purse. "A tankard of ale, and, perhaps, some information."

Marley's eyes glinted appreciatively.

"I encountered a young lady here this morning— a Miss Stafford, I believe. Are you acquainted with her?"

"Not acquainted, so to speak, but I know who you mean. A fine lady, she is."

"Then you can tell me where I can find her?"

"Nothing easier." Marley chuckled. His broad girth, a testament to his wife's fine cooking, quivered beneath his apron. "She lives with her aunt and uncle at the vicarage in Lower Thatchwood. Just follow High Street south across the bridge. Anyone on the other side can show you where the Trents live."

"Thank you," Damian murmured, and passed him the folded notes.

Marley deftly palmed them, but stood hesitating for a moment. "I don't know what you be wanting with Miss Stafford, but maybe I should drop a hint in your ear."

Damian's heavy brows rose inquisitively.

"It's like this, sir. Her uncle, Reverend Mr. Trent, he's a good man, but particular like. Don't hold

47

with no nonsense, 'specially when it comes to his ladies. Keeps them close at home, you see?"

"I do, indeed, and thank you for the warning. I shall bear it in mind."

Marley might have said more, but two men entered the taproom, large, thirsty fellows who called at once for the barkeep. Marley hurried off to serve them, and Damian, reclining in his chair, observed the men. He had the feeling he'd seen them somewhere before.

The older of the pair, a redhead with a receding hairline and arms the size of tree stumps, drained his tankard without pausing for breath, then wiped his mouth on his sleeve. He thumped the counter with a meaty fist until Marley refilled his drink.

The younger man, distinguished by a thatch of dark brown hair and a grizzly beard, drank his ale more slowly. He set the tankard down and motioned for Marley to come closer.

"You had any strangers in here of late?"

"Just yourselves and Mr. Croyden over there," the proprietor answered nervously. The pair looked to be trouble, and he didn't need that sort in his taproom.

Following his gaze, the fellow glanced at Damian, then back to the innkeeper. "Thing is, we're seeking a man who cheated at cards—took a pile of money that rightly don't belong to him. Tall lad, blond hair, blue eyes."

Marley shook his head. "Can't say as I've seen anyone like him about. More ale?"

"Set these gentlemen up again, Marley," Damian said as he rose and sauntered over. When the pair looked up, he drawled. "I do not mean to intrude, but I could not help overhearing your conversation,

48

and if there is one thing that I cannot abide, it is a Captain Sharp. Drink up, gentlemen. I think I may be able to assist you."

"You seen such a fellow?"

Damian nodded. "Regrettably so. Yesterday—about twenty-five miles south of here, in a small village near Derby. The axle broke on my curricle, you see, and I had to abide there until they found a blacksmith to mend it. I found it extremely vexing. You understand how it is when one is forced to wait for an intolerable time?"

"Lord save us from coxcombs," the redhead muttered into his tankard, but his partner elbowed him in the ribs. "Yeah, so you saw this fellow?"

"I have every reason to believe so. There I was with time on my hands when this man, whom I perceived to be a gentleman, joined me at the inn. He introduced himself as Mr. Reynolds . . . or was it Reynald? Well, no matter. The point is, he suggested we engage in a game of piquet. I lost forty pounds, and though I did not realize it at the time, I see clearly now that he must have cheated."

"Well, thanks, Mr. . . . ?"

"Croyden," Damian responded with a deep bow. "Edward Croyden at your service. I do hope you catch the scoundrel."

"You can count on it," the younger man said, and drained his tankard. "Come on, Turk. We've a long ride ahead of us."

The redhead rose reluctantly. He appeared tired, sweaty, and frustrated. "Maybe we oughta wait—"

"We're not being paid to wait. Are you coming, or should I tell his bleeding lordship you couldn't handle the job?"

Grumbling, the pair strode out the door. Damian

watched them leave, well satisfied. His brother would have been proud of him for sending them on a wild-goose chase, but what the devil had Harry done to set this pair on his trail?

Chapter 4

Late Tuesday afternoon, Jonathan Trent stepped into his home, eager for a word with his wife. He was a short man, of such slender build that his coats hung untidily from his narrow shoulders, and due to his nearsightedness, were frequently blotched with stains. His thick spectacles perched on his prominent nose like a hen on a roost. Combined with his balding head, which he made no attempt to hide beneath a wig, he presented a rather odd appearance. However, he was a peaceful man, devout in his beliefs, and if one looked closely, one could see the kindness and intelligence shining in his round brown eyes.

Jonathan was deeply and eternally grateful to his pretty wife, who, despite his obvious shortcomings, had chosen to honor him with her hand, and had further enriched his life with two beautiful daughters. It occasionally troubled his soul that neither his wife nor daughters shared his spiritual devotion, but he consoled himself with the knowledge that it was the Lord's will, and retreated to his library.

Unfortunately, even that sanctuary had been denied to him since the arrival of a letter from his sister-in-law in London, offering to sponsor the girls to a Season in Town. Emily had positively plagued him about the matter, although she knew he disapproved of Town life—the low morals, the gossip, and the endless preoccupation with frivolous pursuits.

A dozen times a day she would interrupt his work to present some new argument. She reminded him that they had met at a ball in Town, and without such harmless diversions, they would never have married. A Season was, she maintained, the only way their daughters would have an opportunity to meet eligible gentlemen. Thomasina was already nineteen and still unwed. Her point was well taken, and Jonathan had been unable to gainsay her.

But today providence had seen fit to drop a most estimable young man right in their midst. A gentleman well educated, of superior intellect, and while not precisely handsome, he appeared sufficiently distinguished to throw Thomasina and Theresa into fits of ecstasy. Jonathan had hurried home, eager to share his news.

He found his wife and daughters ensconced on the settee in the parlor, their heads bent over a magazine, and so engrossed in their chatter, they did not hear him enter.

"A very pretty picture," he remarked from the doorway.

Emily rose at once, flushing guiltily at being caught in such idleness. She came forward with hands outstretched to greet her husband. "I did not expect you to return so soon, sir."

"As we are to have a guest for dinner, I thought it best to come warn you."

"A guest! Who, Papa?" Thomasina asked curiously, for since the squire had left the village, they rarely entertained.

"Probably only Mrs. Caldwalder," Theresa murmured disdainfully. No one interesting, in her opinion, ever came to the vicarage. She wished her father would leave so she could return to looking at the fashion plates in the magazine Aunt Caroline had sent.

"Are you so worldly now that you despise a visit from Mrs. Caldwalder?" Jonathan asked sadly. "I would hope that my daughters would welcome any person to our home with Christian kindness."

Thomasina pinched her sister for her careless remark. If Papa got started on one of his sermons, he would lecture them for an hour or more, and they would all feel wretched by the time he was done for having disappointed him.

Emily frowned at her youngest daughter, then attempted to soothe her husband. "Theresa spoke thoughtlessly, as she is prone to do, but do not be vexed, Jonathan, for you know she does not mean half what she says."

"I pray she does not, but I fear one day this childish habit of not guarding her tongue will lead her into grief."

"She will outgrow it," Emily replied firmly. "Now, if I am to be prepared, you must tell me whom you have invited. I know it is not Helen Caldwalder, for Candace told me she is in bed with the ague, the poor dear. However, I have sent her a restorative and hope to hear better of her within a day or two."

"Where is Candace?" he asked, glancing about the snug room. "Has she not returned from her calls?"

"Not yet, but she intended to visit Mrs. Bellweather, so I am not concerned. You know how she ... that is, she so much enjoys a visit from Candace."

"Indeed," Jonathan agreed, a hint of amusement in his brown eyes, for he knew very well his wife had been about to say that Mrs. Bellweather latched on to visitors with the tenacity of a bulldog. But he did not tease her, only remarking casually, "Well, I do hope she returns in time to change her dress before our guest arrives. I believe she will wish to look her best for Mr. Croyden."

Emily shook her head. "I do not know the name. . . ."

"And how should you, my dear? He is a stranger who stopped at the church only to inquire the way to Epsom Hall."

"The hall? But the squire is not in residence."

"No, nor ever likely to be again. The property has come on the market, and Mr. Croyden told me he is considering buying the hall on behalf of his younger brother, who will require a suitable residence when he weds."

"And Mr. Croyden? Is he married?"

"I knew you would ask," he replied, this time definitely smiling. "The answer is no, but if you are thinking of our daughters, I must warn you that the gentleman is not the sort to be attracted to chattering females who speak without thinking. I own I was most impressed with him. You will hardly credit it, my dear, but he attended Magdalen College at Oxford."

Theresa and Thomasina exchanged knowing looks. Any gentleman who not only impressed their father with his intellect, but who had attended his college, was unlikely to be the sort they longed to meet.

Emily, however, had other notions. The moment her husband retired to the library to work on his sermon, she issued a series of sharp orders to her daughters. Both were to wash their hair at once, and Theresa to wrap hers in papers to induce a bit of curl in her lamentably straight tresses. Thomasina was instructed to smooth a bit of Milk of Roses on her face to improve her complexion, and then to rest until it was time to dress for dinner.

"But, Mama," Theresa objected, "Mr. Croyden must be near Papa's age and can have no interest in meeting us."

"Perhaps," Emily conceded, "but he is obviously a man of some wealth if he is thinking of buying the hall, and you heard Papa say he has a younger brother."

"But he must be—"

"Enough, young lady, or I shall begin to think Papa is correct in believing that you are not sensible enough to be trusted for a Season in London."

"Oh, Mama, pray do not say so."

"You leave me little choice when you waste my time with such foolishness. Now, off with you both. And remember, my dears, if you wish your papa to relent and allow you to visit your Aunt Caroline, you must show him how prettily behaved you can be when in the presence of company."

Candace arrived at the vicarage to find the household thrown into a flurry of preparation. Aunt Emily, who normally would have required an accounting of her morning, was too busy conferring with Cook to spare Candace more than a passing glance. Jenny, the maid of all work employed by the Trents to do the heavy cleaning, had the carpets outside, beating them clean, and Mary, the housemaid, was busy turning out the drawing room.

Candace passed the small library where her uncle habitually worked, thankful to see the door closed. She hurried up to the room she shared with Thomasina and found her cousin immersed in a hip bath, an unusual enough sight at that hour to cause her to stare.

"Good heavens, are we expecting a visit from the queen?"

"Only a gentleman Papa met at the church," Thomasina replied. "He is invited to dinner, and we are all to be on our best behavior. Mama thinks it may help persuade Papa to permit our visit to Aunt Caroline."

"I think it will take more than a show of manners to change Uncle Jonathan's mind," Candace said, hanging up her cloak.

"Hand me that towel, please," Thomasina requested as she rinsed the soap from her skin and prepared to step out of the tub. "Candace, will you help me with my hair?"

"If you wish."

"Mama said you arrange it much nicer than I do. Oh, and she wants us all to wear our silk gowns."

Candace could not believe she'd heard correctly. The new dresses, done up by the village dressmaker in the latest style depicted in the fashion plates, were an extravagance. Aunt Emily had ordered one for each of the girls, paying for them out of her carefully saved pin money. Completed a month ago, the pretty dresses had been set aside in anticipation of the London trip.

There was no one in the neighborhood whom Aunt Emily would deem worthy of honoring in such a manner. With a feeling of foreboding, Candace asked lightly, "Who is this gentleman that we must so impress him? The archbishop, perhaps?"

Thomasina laughed. "Even better, according to Mama. None of us has yet seen him, but he has a younger brother and is considering buying the hall for him when he weds. You know Mama. She has not even met Mr. Croyden, but already she is making plans, for obviously he is a man of some wealth."

"Mr. Croyden?" Candace asked shakily, her heart sinking as her worst fear was confirmed.

Thomasina, after slipping into a dressing gown, was preoccupied with drying her hair and did not see her cousin's pale face. She chattered on, unaware that Candace did not hear a word that was said. Then Theresa entered the room, and any hope of a few moments' quiet reflection was lost.

Candace helped her cousins dress, arranged their hair, and complimented them on their gowns, but her mind was occupied with more pressing concerns. Her practicality told her it could not be mere coincidence that her uncle had met a gentleman named Croyden—it had to be the same stranger who had accosted her that morning. Would he mention their meeting?

She wondered if she should not go down and confess the truth to Uncle Jonathan, even if it meant betraying Harry. Her uncle would be gravely saddened by her conduct, but at least she could warn him that Mr. Croyden was an unprincipled liar. He was not here to buy the hall, but to search for Harry Reynald. Candace was halfway to the door when she found she lacked the moral courage to face her uncle.

She remained in her room, hoping vainly that something would occur to prevent what she felt must surely be a disastrous evening. She dressed slowly, unaware that the delicate green silk slip, worn beneath an overdress of white net, flattered her slender figure a great deal more than the loose-fitting gowns she customarily wore. Or that the steam from the bath had caused tiny, dark tendrils to curl softly about her face. Had she glanced in the looking-glass, she would have noticed that the color of her gown complemented her eyes, turning them a soft greenish gray that was most becoming. But all Candace could think of was facing Mr. Croyden.

A soft tap on the door startled her. She turned around nervously, but it was only Theresa. "Mama sent me to see what is keeping you—oh, how nice you look."

"Thank you," she answered absently. "Has . . . has Mr. Croyden arrived?"

"No, but Mama wants us in the drawing room beforehand. What a lot of bustle. One would think the prince regent himself was coming to dine instead of just Papa's fusty friend."

"You may be surprised," Candace cautioned as she followed her cousin to the door. She would not describe Croyden as fusty. Dangerous, rugged, unprincipled, but not fusty.

"Listen! Good heavens, that must be his carriage," Theresa cried. "Oh, do hurry."

Candace watched her cousin dart down the hall and disappear around the stairs. She took a deep calming breath, murmured a brief prayer, and then slowly followed.

She was halfway down the steps when the knocker sounded. Uncle Jonathan answered the door himself, a mark of high distinction he rarely conferred on guests, and a moment later Edward Croyden walked into the house.

From Candace's vantage point he seemed to fill the entryway, making her uncle look small and somehow fragile. It was not just his height, for he stood only a few inches above average, that made the difference. He was simply the sort of man who commanded everyone's attention when he entered a room. Candace set it down to his natural arrogance.

As if sensing her presence, he glanced up. Her gaze met his, and for a moment Candace could do nothing but stare into the smoky depths of his eyes.

Jonathan, noticing his guest's distraction, turned his head and saw his niece. Her appearance gave him pause. It could have been her mother standing so hesitantly on the stairs. Diana had looked much the same when she'd married Charles. Quite beautiful, really . . . recollecting himself, he blinked, then called up, "Candace, my dear, do come meet our distinguished visitor."

She walked slowly down the stairs but could not break the spell that held her gaze locked with Edward Croyden's. She barely heard the introduction, but she was intensely aware of his gloved hand touching hers, and of the sound of his voice. Deep, rich, civilized tones—a far cry from the angry notes she had heard him speak that morning.

She responded somehow and then, at her uncle's behest, led the way into the drawing room. She had a few moments in which to compose herself while Uncle Jonathan introduced Mr. Croyden to the rest of the family. She observed him bowing elegantly to her aunt, somehow looking every inch the perfect gentleman, though he was not dressed appropriately for an evening call.

His claret riding coat, which she admitted suited him extraordinarily well, should have been replaced by a formal cutaway coat with white waistcoat, and his high Hessian boots, had he any pretensions to being a gentleman, exchanged for silk stockings and pumps.

Mr. Croyden, seeming to read her mind, apologized to her aunt. "I hope you will forgive my informality, but I am traveling light and had not anticipated the need for formal attire."

"Do not give it a thought, sir," Emily gushed. "We do not stand on formality here. Indeed, I pray you will not think us hopelessly provincial for dining at six."

He laughed. "I am thankful for it. We do not keep Town hours at Deerpark, and when I am in London, I find I am starving by eight or nine."

"Well, we set a simple table," Jonathan told him, "but I think you will find it superior to what you are likely to receive at the Boar's Head. You are more than welcome to take potluck with us any evening you wish."

Candace stared at her uncle in disbelief. He seldom invited anyone to dine, and for him to extend an open invitation was unheard of.

Mary tapped on the door and announced dinner was served. Mr. Croyden rose at once, gallantly offered his arm to her aunt, and escorted her from the room. Uncle Jonathan followed with Thomasina, leaving Candace with her younger cousin.

"Is he not divine?" Theresa whispered. "All dark

and ruggedly handsome—he sends shivers down my back every time he glances in my direction. I vow he is just like one of those heroes in Mrs. Radcliffe's books."

More like the villain, Candace thought, but made no comment. She sat through the turtle soup and the fish, watching Mr. Croyden charm her aunt and her cousins with practiced ease. Over the roasted fowl he spoke with her uncle on the divisions within the Church of England, and sounded surprisingly knowledgeable. And when Mary handed round cherry-water ices and fresh strawberries, he talked about the hall and the improvements he would undertake if he were to buy it.

Candace listened, amazed. Had she not known his true reason for being in Lower Thatchwood, she would have believed Croyden to be a respectable gentlemen, interested only in buying Squire Epsom's estate for his brother. But she knew the truth and silently seethed at his deception.

Finally, unable to tolerate his cool assurance any longer, Candace dared to quiz him. "I am surprised, sir, that you would wish your brother to live in so remote an area."

"It may be remote, but it is certainly invested with considerable beauty," he replied smoothly, and smiled meaningfully at her aunt and cousins.

Theresa simpered and Thomasina blushed, but Candace would not be put off so easily. "Tell us about this brother of yours—you did say you are considering buying the hall for him, I believe?"

"Candace! Really, my dear," Emily protested with an embarrassed glance at their guest. "You quite sound as though you doubt Mr. Croyden."

61

Damian laughed. "As well she should, Mrs. Trent. I am, after all, a stranger in your midst."

"Well, I hope you will not consider yourself as such for long, Mr. Croyden," Emily declared. "I may not have lived in London for some years, but I do believe myself sufficiently well acquainted with the Quality to recognize a true gentleman when I see one."

"Thank you," he murmured, and turned to Candace. "What was it you wished to know, Miss Stafford?"

"I was merely curious about your brother, sir," she replied, wondering why no one else seemed to notice the way his eyes mocked her. "I do not believe I heard you mention his name."

"Harry," he answered with a straight face, though devilment glinted in his eyes. "Harry Reynald."

Candace, in the act of sipping a glass of lemonade, nearly choked. The audacity of the man! She set her glass down, took a deep breath, and replied as calmly as possible, "How odd that you have different surnames."

"Not at all," he said, and safe in the knowledge that she would not believe him, explained, "We are merely half brothers."

Jonathan nodded his head in approval. "Then it is most commendable that you are willing to provide so generously for him."

"I am, but whether he will accept my help remains to be seen. Since Harry's father died, he has been involved in a number of scrapes, nothing serious, but I am sure you'll understand that as his guardian, I am somewhat concerned. Of course, Harry resents what he considers to be interference on my part."

"Naturally," Jonathan agreed. "In my experience, young men are seldom willing to be ruled by wiser heads."

"What young men?" Theresa whispered to Candace.

Mr. Croyden appeared not to have heard, and smiled gratefully at his host. "You do understand, then? Harry's a good lad, and I have every hope that once he weds, he will settle down and accept his responsibilities."

"I am sure he will," Emily said. Then, with a pretense at casualness that fooled no one, she asked, "Is he betrothed, or perhaps you have a particular young lady in mind?"

"I regret to say my brother has not met anyone yet capable of engaging his affections. . . . Of course, he has not had the advantage of meeting such lovely young ladies as I have this evening—at least, I do not believe so," he added, looking directly at Candace.

She met his gaze boldly and lifted her chin defiantly. "I am very sure I have never met *your* brother, sir." Her aunt and her cousins might accept Croyden's blatant flattery, but she had only contempt for a man who could lie so fluently—and so convincingly. He responded easily to something her aunt said, but Candace fancied she detected a warning look in his dark eyes. A look which, as Theresa said, sent shivers down one's back.

When at last her aunt rose, Candace thought she would have a respite. However, instead of sitting at the table with her uncle, or stepping outside for a smoke, Mr. Croyden chose to join the ladies in the drawing room. He was enthusiastic in his praise of the meal, a performance entirely overdone in Candace's opinion, but her aunt positively glowed at his words. She echoed her husband's invitation that Mr. Croyden must join them for dinner whenever he wished.

"You are too kind, Mrs. Trent, but if I accept, you must allow me to repay your hospitality. I understand there is an assembly room in Heptonstall with dances every Wednesday. Perhaps you will permit me to escort you and your daughters, and your niece, of course."

Candace waited for her uncle to politely decline the scheme, but when Emily looked to him for guidance, he nodded his acquiescence. "It seems an unexceptional plan, but are you certain, Mr. Croyden, that you wish to escort so many females?"

"An embarrassment of riches? Perhaps you are right, sir, though it poses a problem." He turned to Emily with an engaging smile, and lifted his hands helplessly. "I am so new to the neighborhood, I would not know whom else to ask. However, if you would be kind enough to arrange a small party, it would not only give me the opportunity to repay your hospitality, but allow me the chance to meet some of the young people my brother would be socializing with were I to buy the hall."

Emily laughed. "I would willingly do so, sir, but unfortunately there is a scarcity of young people in Lower Thatchwood. 'Tis one of the drawbacks of our neighborhood."

"How strange," he murmured, and flicked a glance in Candace's direction. "I could have sworn I heard the proprietress at the inn speaking about a group of young people getting up a picnic today."

"In Thatchwood? You must be mistaken, Mr. Croyden. I would have heard of such, I assure you.

64

However, I believe we may persuade Sir Bonamy's son to join us, and Mr. Fairgood, who farms an exceptionally large holding just north of town." She lowered her voice and confided, "He is rather sweet on my niece."

"It sounds an excellent party, and I shall leave everything in your hands. Shall we settle on Wednesday a week, then?"

At the mention of a picnic, Candace, not knowing where to look, had lowered her eyes, but she could not control the delicate blush that tinted her cheeks. *Unprincipled rogue,* she thought.

She had been helpless to stop Mr. Croyden from worming his way into the family, and now it looked as though she would be responsible for foisting an unconscionable liar off on the neighborhood. She must think of some way of getting rid of him without betraying herself or Harry.

She racked her brain but still had not thought of a solution, when Mr. Croyden stood to take his leave. He bowed over Thomasina's hand, and said something to set her blushing, then teasingly told Theresa she must save a dance for him.

When he reached Candace, he turned slightly so that his back was to the others, his words for her ears alone. "My dear Miss Stafford, do not look so downcast. If you are fearful I shall fail you on Wednesday, you need not be. I always keep my word. Did I not say we would meet again?"

"But I have no desire to do so," she murmured low enough so that her aunt could not hear.

"Then you need only tell me where I can find Harry. Think on it, my dear."

Chapter 5

Candace spent a wretched night, tormented by dreams of Edward Croyden. His face, with his dark, smoky eyes, haunted her. She suffered visions of him denouncing her to her uncle, visions of him finding and brutally attacking Harry ... and rather unsettling visions of dancing with him at the assembly in Heptonstall, held captive while he questioned her. She awoke, more tired than rested, and imagined she could still feel the strength of his arms around her.

She dressed quickly, eager to escape the memories of her dreams, and hurried down to the breakfast room. The family was already seated, and she could hear her cousins' lively chatter from the hall. Candace slipped in and took her seat.

She sat quietly, allowing the conversation to flow around her as she tried to think of an excuse that would allow her to see Harry. It was a moment before she realized that silence had fallen and everyone was looking in her direction.

Uncle Jonathan smiled at her. "It is gratifying to see that one member of my family is not so given over to the pursuit of frivolous pleasure that she can speak of little else."

Theresa and Thomasina flushed at the gentle rebuke, and Aunt Emily protested, "Now, Jonathan, 'tis only natural that our daughters are a trifle excited. They are good girls, but they have had so few occasions to socialize that it would be surprising if they did not look forward to the assembly with an unusual degree of anticipation."

Theresa, seated beside Candace, pinched her sharply beneath the cover of the table linen, while Thomasina glared at her.

"It is not the assembly I object to, but this preoccupation with it to the exclusion of all else," Jonathan said sadly. "I am certain Candace will also enjoy the excursion, but she does not behave as though it were the only matter of importance."

"Thank you, Uncle, but I do not deserve to be singled out. If I seem less excited than my cousins, 'tis only because I awoke with a bit of the headache this morning."

"Oh, my dear, I do hope you are not becoming ill," Emily said, looking at her niece with concern. "Perhaps you should rest this morning. I could fix you a restorative—"

"I am certain I shall feel better directly," Candace interrupted quickly. She had tasted her aunt's restoratives before and had no wish to repeat the experience.

Her uncle nodded. "It is never good to coddle oneself. Some fresh air and exercise will no doubt set you right. Indeed, I was hoping I might persuade you to ride over and visit Mrs. Caldwalder this morning. The poor soul is still grieving for her husband, and some companionship would do her good."

"I would be pleased to," Candace murmured. Mrs. Caldwalder lived near the hall and the visit would provide the perfect excuse to slip away and see Harry.

"Theresa? Thomasina? Do you not wish to accompany your cousin?"

"Oh, pray, Papa, do not make us," Thomasina pleaded. "I know it is uncharitable of me, but she always wants to tell us about how Mr. Caldwalder died and it—it makes me queasy."

"We must all face our mortality sometime, child. Death is nothing to fear if you have faith in the Lord."

"I know and I do, but to think of poor Mr. Caldwalder choking on a bone and no one even noticing until his head fell into the stew. Mrs. Caldwalder always tells us how when they lifted his head, there were bits of carrots and potatoes—"

"Enough, Thomasina," Emily said with a delicate shudder. "I am sure your father will excuse you. Indeed, I had planned for all three of you to spend the morning sewing—"

"I could go with Candace," volunteered Theresa, who loathed needlepoint even more than visiting the ill.

"I think not," Emily replied with a sharp look that warned her daughter not to argue. "Your skills with a needle leave much to be desired. I believe a morning spent in the sewing room will profit you more than visiting Mrs. Caldwalder."

Candace silently blessed her aunt for insisting her cousin stay home. Theresa's company would have complicated matters dreadfully, and if her younger cousin ever saw Harry, she would be instantly smitten. He was just the sort of young man Theresa would think terribly daring and romantic instead of merely stubbornly foolish, and the unwitting cause of a great deal of trouble.

An hour later Candace tied Garnet's reins to a shrub, then continued on foot to the gamekeeper's hut. She knew not whether to thank the Lord for providing her with an excuse to ride out this morning, or the devil for adding to the deception she was practicing. She cringed inwardly, remembering her uncle's kindness at the breakfast table.

Harry was sitting on the makeshift cot when she entered the cottage, and looked remarkably well, considering his wound. Apparently he'd bathed at the stream, for his blond hair was damp and brushed back off his brow, and the light down on his jaw she'd noticed yesterday had been shaved clean.

He stood up and greeted her carelessly, "Good day, Miss Stafford. I was hoping you would come, for I am fair ravenous. What have you brought me?"

"Why, nothing," she faltered. "Surely, you cannot have eaten all I brought yesterday?"

He grinned, unabashed. "Most of it. There's not much else to do."

Candace shook her head. "I am pleased your appetite is not impaired, for that must mean you are on the mend, but with the best will in the world, I cannot afford to continue feeding you. I used the last of my allowance to purchase the basket, and I cannot take anything from the vicarage or my aunt will notice."

His good-natured grin disappeared. Money had seldom been a problem, and to be without it now was proving extremely tedious. "What are we to do, then?"

"We?" she asked, raising her brows.

"You are the one who insisted on helping me when I advised you to leave me alone—surely, you do not mean to desert me now?"

"I suggested you apply to my uncle for assistance, but you would not hear of it. I do not know what else to advise, but you cannot continue to stay here."

Harry's guileless blue eyes widened in alarm. "Let's not be hasty. Granted this is not the sort of accommodations I prefer, and under other circumstances I would be quite willing to leave, but I didn't think you'd be so heartless as to evict me. What ails you this morning, Miss Stafford?"

Exasperated, she faced him, hands on her hips. "What ails me, sir, is that Mr. Croyden—you do remember Mr. Croyden, the gentleman who is looking for you?—well, he somehow managed to meet my uncle, and as a consequence dined at the vicarage last night. It was a most unsettling experience."

Damian dining with the vicar? What the devil was his brother up to? Harry gestured toward the table. "Will you sit down, Miss Stafford? Apparently, I am even more indebted to you than I believed."

Slightly mollified, she sat gingerly on the edge of one of the rickety chairs. "I suppose you might as well call me Candace—we cannot continue to stand on formality in such surroundings."

Harry bowed, a trifle awkwardly, but with a trace of his old jauntiness. "I am honored, and I am known to my friends as Harry. We *are* friends, are we not?"

70

"Allies," she conceded, but a hint of a smile curved the corners of her lips as she added, "Harry."

"Thank you. Now, about Croyden—can you not continue to declaim all knowledge of me? There is really nothing he can do if you stand firm."

She shook her head. "I wish it were that simple, but he could tell my uncle he saw me in Upper Thatchwood with a picnic basket. He hinted at it last night. He is . . . he is persecuting me," she said, lifting her hands in a helpless gesture as she searched for words to explain the way Mr. Croyden made her feel. "The man is relentless—and he knows, Harry. He knows I have seen you. He even had the audacity to tell my uncle that you are his brother."

"Did he now? That is interesting."

"I taxed him with why you have different names, and he quickly amended his story and said you were half brothers. But what frightens me most is that Croyden feels certain I can tell him where to find you, and I am convinced he will not leave me alone until I do so."

"Perhaps if you were to tell him I was here but that I have left?"

"I doubt he would believe me, but—if you were to really leave? Your arm looks much better, and if you just continued on your journey . . ." Her words trailed off as Harry sadly shook his head.

"Much as I should like to oblige you, there's a slight problem. My horse is at the livery stable, and I haven't the funds to redeem him."

"Why on earth did you leave him there?" she demanded, vexed to learn of this new problem. "I should think anyone with a grain of sense would want to keep his horse near him in such a situation."

"I assure you, it was not by choice," Harry mumbled. "I passed out and tumbled from the saddle. Majestic wandered into the road, and when I came to, some fellows from town had caught him up. *They* took him to the stable."

"Oh, I see. Well, how much do you suppose you need to reclaim him?"

Harry shrugged, then quickly crossed to the window and stared intently at the woods surrounding the hut. His hand reached for the silver dueling pistol resting on a makeshift wooden shelf.

"What is it?" Candace whispered, alarmed.

"I thought I heard something, but 'tis just a squirrel." He replaced the pistol and leaned against the wall. "How much do I need? Well, as near as I can figure, about six thousand two hundred and ten pounds should be sufficient."

"Harry, do be serious. I may not know much about stables, but I do know they cannot charge such an enormous sum for merely boarding a horse."

"No—ten pounds should be enough for the livery. But I owe a neighbor two hundred pounds for damage to his property, and I need six thousand to cover a gambling debt."

"Six thousand?" Candace gasped, her eyes wide with disbelief. "You lost six thousand pounds gambling? Why, that is nearly enough to feed and clothe a family for a year. How *could* you lose so much?"

"Very easily, apparently. Truth to tell, I don't remember much about the evening. I rather suspect my drink was drugged and the gentleman cheated,"

he said, striving for an air of nonchalant unconcern.

Despite the challenging way he stuck out his
chin, and the bravado in his voice, Candace sensed
Harry was near desperate. She sought to somehow
comfort him. "Well, if that is true, I should think
you need not pay the debt."

"I must pay it—I signed a vowel, Candace. 'Tis a
debt of honor."

"But if the gentleman drugged you and cheated?
Surely that must make a difference?"

Harry sighed. "Only if I could prove it, which I
cannot. It would be his word against mine, and the
gentleman is of most noble birth."

Candace sighed and looked down at her hands.
The code of gentlemen was beyond her understanding. Lord Blackstone could elope with a married
lady and not be thought ill of by the nobility, but
the woman would be beyond redemption. A member of the peerage could drink himself into oblivion
and still be readily forgiven. Young lords could risk
the lives of stagecoach passengers in their foolish
races, and it was set down to mere high spirits. But
no man who claimed to be a gentleman could welsh
on a gambling debt, or he'd be shunned by Society.

"You must think I am a pretty ramshackle fellow
to have gotten in such a fix."

She glanced up at him. "No, just foolish. But how
can you hope to raise such a sum? Perhaps if you
were to explain to your family—"

"I cannot," he said with such firmness, there was
no arguing with him. "I left home because of an argument with my . . . my family. They think I am
rather a worthless sort, and I'm beginning to believe they are right. They have hauled me out of

scrapes all my life, but this time I vowed I would not run to them for help. I got myself into this bind, and I must do whatever is necessary to extricate myself. Only . . . only 'tis proving a trifle more difficult than I had imagined."

"Then what are you going to do? I suspect you have some scheme in mind."

"My grandfather left me a small estate near York, and his string of hunters. If I can get there, I can sell the horses for enough to cover my debts, but I need your help, Candace. Right now I cannot hope to pay the livery—I haven't so much as a sixpence—but neither can I leave without Majestic. Under the circumstances, there is only one thing to do."

Candace stood. "Harry, if you are thinking of stealing your horse, I will have no part of it. I would far rather you approach my uncle. He will be angry at first, but I know he will do all in his power to help you."

"I suppose I deserve that you think so little of me, but I have not yet sunk to thievery," he said, drawing himself up to his full height. "And I will not go to your uncle. That would really land you in the briars. As it is, I never should have allowed you to become involved in my affairs."

"Well, you did try to warn me off," she owned, touched by the misery in his eyes. "But how else will you get Majestic?"

He slowly drew off the large emerald ring he customarily wore on his right hand, and handed it to her. "I want you to take this and sell it for whatever you can get. I'm told it's a very fine stone . . . it belonged to my father."

"Oh, Harry, must you?" she asked with quick sympathy.

He smiled ruefully, then turned to stare out the window again. "I fear it is my only choice. Perhaps later I can buy the ring back. I don't wish to involve you more than necessary, but will you try to sell it for me?" he asked, his voice sounding strangely muffled.

Candace sighed as she glanced down at the heavy gold band and square-cut emerald. "Of course I will try, but there is no one in Thatchwood who would buy such a thing. Unless . . . do you think Mr. Croyden would—"

"No!" Harry interrupted furiously as he turned to face her. "On no account must you show him that ring. Croyden knows me—he would recognize it in an instant."

"You do not trust him, then?" she asked.

"At present I trust no one save yourself. Promise me you will not show him that ring."

"Very well, but it means I must somehow contrive to visit Heptonstall, and that will not be easy."

"Can you not simply tell your uncle that you wish to go shopping for ribbons or something? My cousins are always running in to Town for hats and gewgaws."

Candace laughed, and when he stared at her in surprise, she laughed harder. "Oh, Harry, 'tis obvious you have never lived in a vicarage," she explained when she caught her breath. "We do not *run in to town* for gewgaws or anything else. Indeed, we rarely go anywhere, and a visit to Heptonstall is something of an occasion."

He could not conceive of it and gazed at her in

astonishment. "But what do you do about dresses and such?"

"We make most of our clothes, or, in very exceptional circumstances, engage the village dressmaker."

"I see," he replied, letting his gaze run over her ill-fitting muslin day dress.

Candace smiled, knowing he was too kind to remark that her lack of expertise with a needle showed. "Never mind, I will manage something. For now, we must think how best to feed you. Do you fish?"

Damian emerged from his hiding place beneath the window of the gamekeeper's hut and rubbed his aching back. After crouching in the shrubbery for the better part of an hour, he felt stiff and sore, but he had not dared to move. Harry, blast the boy, had excellent hearing. He had been drawn to the window in an instant the one time Damian had shifted position.

He glanced toward the path where his brother had disappeared with Miss Stafford and grinned. He would like to see that young lady showing his brother how to fashion a rod from a tree limb, a bit of silk for a line, and a thorn for a hook. But he had to get back to the path and retrieve his horse before Miss Stafford returned.

He left the woods with a lighter heart, relieved to know for certain that his brother was reasonably well. Damian had not been surprised to learn Harry was wounded—he had suspected as much—but Harry, for all he thought he was treading deep water, was in far more trouble than he guessed.

And whether he wished it or not, Damian intended to take a hand in the game.

Paddy was waiting with the horses, as arranged, near the road. "Thought I was going to have to come looking for you," the groom said by way of greeting.

"I did not think I would be so long, but I am certain you will agree the wait was worthwhile," Damian said as he accepted the reins of his horse. With a wide grin that made him look years younger, he added, "Harry is here and well enough."

"I hope you gave him the rough side of your tongue—troublesome boy, worrying the mistress and all," Paddy muttered, but he could not quite hide the relief in his eyes. "Well, tell me now what the pup had to say for himself."

"Actually, I did not speak to him."

Paddy, in the act of mounting, missed his footing and nearly tumbled backward. When he'd regained his balance, he glared at the earl. "You didna' speak to him? We trailed him all this way, and you didna' speak to him?"

"Mount up and I will tell you about it," Damian said. "I wish to be out of these woods before Miss Stafford finds us, but mark the direction. Harry is staying in a cottage roughly a mile north of here."

Damian led the way on the narrow, winding path, and did not speak again until they were on High Street. He slackened his pace then and glanced at his groom, who looked as ominous as a thundercloud about to burst.

"The reason I did not speak to Harry is that he apparently does not want my help."

"That would be a first," Paddy grumbled. "Why not?"

"Perhaps he's growing up at last. He told Miss Stafford that he got himself into this scrape and he means to get himself out of it without running to his family for help."

"May the saints preserve us, the boy's finally showing some sense. But scrape is hardly what I'd call it when the Duke of Cardiff comes banging on the door demanding sixty thousand pounds. 'Tis a ruddy fortune, and the young master will be hard put to lay his hands on so much."

Damian gazed at his groom, then sighed. "Foolish of me, I suppose, but I had thought my interview with Cardiff was private. Were you listening at the door?"

"Not me, gov, but such tidings have a way of getting about. Now, don't be getting on your high horse. You know there ain't a lad or lass in the house that ain't devoted to you and her ladyship."

"Why did you not say something sooner?"

The little groom shrugged. "Figured when you was ready for me to know, you'd say so, but I tell you this much. Ain't one of the lads believing Master Harry would risk so much on the turn of a card."

"Nor do I," Damian said coldly. "I heard Harry tell Miss Stafford that he lost six thousand pounds—not sixty, as Cardiff claimed."

"Blimey! You think the duke doctored Master Harry's note?"

"It's beginning to look that way, and would explain why someone seems determined to ambush my brother."

The groom shivered at the grim look in his lordship's eyes, which boded ill for someone.

Damian pulled up his mount. "You go back to the

village, Paddy. Apparently, a couple of farmers found Majestic wandering in the road and turned him into the livery. See that he is well taken care of, and find a way to assure the stable master that I will make good the bill if his owner does not claim him. Tell him I plan to buy the stallion, if necessary."

"Yes, sir," Paddy answered with unusual meekness. "You're not coming with me?"

"No. I wish to have a word with Miss Stafford first."

Chapter 6

Candace rounded the curve of High Street and saw Edward Croyden cantering toward her. She sighed. She'd warned Harry the man would not easily be avoided, but she had not expected to encounter him again so soon. Thank heavens he had not come along ten minutes earlier and seen her leaving the woods.

She reined in Garnet from her slow-moving trot to barely a walk and waited for Croyden to approach her. He was riding bareheaded this morning, and his dark hair fell over his brow in soft, disordered waves. But even with his hair mussed, he managed to maintain an air of easy superiority. Perhaps it was the way he sat astride his horse, back straight, broad shoulders back—master of all he surveyed.

Despite her dislike of Croyden, she couldn't help comparing him to Jasper Fairgood—much to her suitor's detriment. Poor Jasper. Riding was never a pleasure for him. He crouched over his horse's neck as though he feared the animal would bolt, and habitually clutched the reins so tightly, he had ruined the mouth of several good mares. No matter how hard he tried, he would never ride a horse with the natural grace of a man like Edward Croyden.

"Good day, Miss Stafford," that gentleman greeted her as he reined in alongside her. "I see you make a habit of riding alone."

"I prefer it," she replied pointedly.

"But it is not safe, Miss Stafford. One never knows whom one might encounter," he replied, his gaze raking down the long sweep of her skirt.

Though she longed to kick Garnet into a gallop, Candace sat still. It was too much to hope that Croyden would not notice the mud on her boot from where she had waded in the stream with Harry, but in an effort to divert his attention she replied, "Until your arrival in the village, I rarely encountered anyone. Lower Thatchwood is hardly a metropolis."

"Nevertheless, I cannot deem it wise," he said, smiling at her as though he really cared. "If you wish to indulge in a morning ride, I would be glad to escort you."

"Thank you, but this is not a pleasure jaunt, sir. My uncle asked me to pay a call on one of the parishioners who is in mourning. She lost her husband recently, and she misses his companionship. Uncle Jonathan felt she needed a sympathetic ear." *Oh, Lord, I sound like a babbling idiot,* she thought, and firmly shut her lips against further explanations.

His brows arched and the eyes below glittered with merriment. "How very thoughtful of you. Many ladies I know would resent spending their morning in such a manner."

"If they resent performing an act of simple Christian kindness, perhaps you should choose the company you keep more carefully," she replied.

"Touché," he said, grinning good-naturedly despite her insult. "But I am still all admiration that

you would willingly give up your morning to listen to an old lady air her complaints."

"Calling on parishioners in need is part of my duties at the vicarage."

"Modest, too. Well, 'tis comforting to know there is a sympathetic ear available, should I have need of one."

"I beg your pardon?"

"I said that is comforting—"

"I heard what you said, Mr. Croyden, but apparently you are laboring under a misapprehension. *You* are not one of my uncle's parishioners."

"Ah, but I shall be if I buy the hall, or at least Harry will, and I should think that as a member of his family, I would be entitled to whatever services the local vicar provides."

She longed to wipe the mocking smile off his mouth, and was very nearly provoked into telling him she knew he was not Harry's brother—which was undoubtedly and precisely what Croyden wished her to do.

Biting her lip, she gathered up Garnet's reins, then smiled sweetly. "You are correct, Mr. Croyden, except that it is Uncle Jonathan who calls on the gentlemen in residence. But I am sure he would be delighted to come visit you. Shall I ask him?"

"Thank you, Miss Stafford, but I should hate to put you to so much trouble. I will speak to him myself." The corners of his mouth curved up with irrepressible amusement as he added, "I dine with you this evening."

"Again? My aunt will be extremely flattered."

"But not you, Miss Stafford?"

"My Christian upbringing prohibits me from telling you exactly what I think of you, Mr. Croyden, but *flattered* is not among the adjectives I would choose to describe my feelings. Now, if you will excuse me?"

Before she could nudge Garnet into a trot, he reached out a hand and firmly grasped the mare's bridle. All traces of humor disappeared from his smoky eyes as he looked gravely down at her.

"I intend to remain in Lower Thatchwood as long as Harry is here. I cannot force you to trust me, but I wish you would believe that I mean only to keep him from harm."

Edward Croyden was very persuasive. His deep voice rang with sincerity, and though he towered over her, his presence suddenly seemed more comforting than threatening. For a moment Candace almost believed him. She shifted uncomfortably and felt the weight of Harry's emerald ring in her pocket as it brushed against her thigh. She remembered his vehement insistence that she not say a word to Croyden.

Glancing away from his mesmerizing eyes as a blush suffused her cheeks, she murmured, "I am sure I do not know what you mean."

"And I am very certain that you do, but I will not argue the point. Just remember that if either of you should find yourself at a standstill, you may come to me for help."

He sounded as if he really meant the words, Candace thought, but she hardened her heart against his appeal. Keeping her gaze fixed on the road, she replied coolly, "If you really wish to help me, sir, there is one thing you could do."

"You have only to ask."

"Then please release my mare. I must return to the vicarage."

He instantly dropped his hand and backed his stallion a pace or two. "You see, Miss Stafford? I am yours to command."

Candace snapped the reins, urging Garnet to a trot. Exasperating, insufferable, aggravating man, she thought, and waited to hear the clip of his horse's hooves behind her. She rode twenty paces, her shoulders tensed, alert for any sound, but only a magpie's piercing call broke the silence. When she could stand it no longer, she glanced over her shoulder.

Croyden remained where she'd left him. When he saw her look back, he waved, then turned his stallion in the opposite direction. Relieved, Candace urged Garnet to hurry, wanting to put as much distance as possible between them. She glanced back again, but Edward Croyden had disappeared.

"Good riddance," Candace muttered, but she could not quite stifle the small stab of disappointment she felt. Pitting her wits against Croyden had sharpened all her senses and stirred the blood in her veins. She wished her mare were capable of more than a trot—she suddenly felt like racing the wind. Silly of her, she thought, and patted Garnet's silky neck. Her horse moved with the decorous speed entirely suitable to the niece of a vicar. The mare's pace was almost a reproach.

Candace knew she would do well to remember her position. She was *not* like her mother, and she would not, no matter what Mr. Croyden thought, be easily won over by a few words of flattery and a pair of dark, smoky eyes.

Reluctant to go home, Candace turned her mare into the neatly trimmed drive leading to Mrs. Bellweather's. Although crippled by arthritis now, it was rumored the lady had once been a reigning beauty, and could have married a duke if she had wished. That she chose instead to wed plain Herbert Bellweather so incensed her family, they cut the connection. She had not seen one of her relatives in more than twenty years, but did not appear to regret the loss.

Candace cantered up the drive, admiring the deep red roses that grew in profusion near the cottage. Maude Bellweather had planted and nourished her garden over the years, taking great delight in sending bountiful bouquets to her neighbors. Now she engaged a young boy to tend her flowers, an expense she could ill afford but insisted upon. She was fond of saying she would rather go without food than see her garden suffer neglect.

Candace sometimes suspected the old lady employed a succession of garden boys because they provided her with someone to talk to. On more than one occasion Candace had arrived to find the latest lad in the cottage, looking uncomfortably out of place as he sat gingerly on the edge of a needlepoint cushion, a delicate goblet of lemonade clutched in his grimy fingers, while he listened to Mrs. Bellweather reminisce about her youthful days in London.

Candace glanced around the yard, but young Darby, the latest lad, was nowhere in sight. She rapped on the door, then waited patiently. A few moments later she heard the tap of Mrs. Bellweather's cane moving slowly across the floor, saw the edge of the curtain on the wide front window twitch, and then the door was thrown open.

"Candace, my dear, do come in," Maude said, a smile of pleased surprise adding to the abundance of wrinkles in the old lady's lined face. She hesitated a second, her small, lively eyes looking puzzled. "Was I expecting you?"

"No," Candace assured her. "I called on Mrs. Caldwalder, and since I had to pass your cottage on the way home, I thought I would stop to see if you were in need of anything."

Maude chuckled. "I need so much, the Lord has grown weary of listening to my petitions, but I doubt if you can provide me with a new set of ears or pair of eyes."

"I wish I could," Candace replied sincerely.

Maude stepped closer and peered up at her visitor's face. Even with cataracts blinding her vision, she could see Candace looked unusually tired. "Come in, child, come in. Surely you can stay long enough to have a cup of tea?"

"Thank you, Mrs. Bellweather, but I do not wish to trouble you—"

"Nonsense. Talking is one of the few pleasures left to me, and the pot's already on the boil. Annie set the tray up before she left," Maude said, referring to the village girl who came three days a week to clean the cottage.

Candace followed the tiny white-haired figure as she moved slowly down the dark hall to an informal sitting room on the south side of the house. She knew Mrs. Bellweather preferred the sunny room to the more formal parlor at the rear. She said it was because it overlooked the gardens, but Candace had little doubt the room was favored because of its commanding view of High Street. Mrs. Bellweather spent most of her time in the chair positioned in front of the tall windows, and as a consequence, little occurred in Lower Thatchwood without her knowledge.

"I heard you had a guest at the vicarage last evening," Maude commented as she settled herself in the high-backed wing chair.

Startled, Candace nodded. Then she remembered that Annie was half sister to Jenny, who would have certainly told her about the preparations for a dinner guest. She smiled at Mrs. Bellweather. "Did Annie tell you who?"

"No, but she said your aunt turned the house upside down. Would it be that young man I've seen riding past here several times of late?"

"I do not think your eyesight is bad at all," Candace teased, accepting a delicate china cup full of weakly brewed tea.

"It's not what it used to be," Maude replied, shaking her head sadly. "I could tell he's tall, and sits a horse well, but not what he looked like—not even with my opera glasses. Is he handsome?"

Unaccountably, Candace felt herself blushing. "He is not ... unattractive, I suppose, in a rough sort of way."

Maude laughed. "Like that, is it? Got a soft spot for him?"

"Oh, no, not at all," Candace declared vehemently. "Indeed, I would prefer not to see him ever again."

"Then send the gentleman around—or ask your uncle to. Jonathan Trent is not the sort to abide a young man forcing his attentions on you."

Candace sighed. "I wish it were that simple, but Mr. Croyden has not done or said anything to which I could object. I just ... I do not trust him, but Uncle Jonathan thinks highly of him. He invited Mr. Croyden to dine with us whenever he wishes, and my aunt is more than agreeable. Even my cousins think he is top-of-the-trees."

"Croyden? I do not believe I know the name—where's he from? Who are his people?"

"He mentioned an estate somewhere north of London that he calls Deerpark, and he attended the same college at Oxford as Uncle Jonathan, but more than that I do not know."

"Deerpark," Maude murmured, her brow furrowed. "I recollect a house by that name . . . but I do not suppose it can be the same. What brings Mr. Croyden to Lower Thatchwood?"

"He told Uncle Jonathan he intends to buy the hall for his younger brother when he weds."

"Well, that explains Emily's interest," Maude said with a deep-throated laugh. "If he can afford the hall, he's well breeched. She probably intends your Mr. Croyden for one of her girls."

"Not him—the younger brother." Candace smiled at the older woman's astuteness, then added soberly, "I only hope they are not taking him too much on his word."

"I shouldn't worry. Your uncle is a shrewd judge of character, my dear. In all the years I have known him, he has seldom been proved wrong." Maude hesitated, then reached across and took Candace's hand in her own. "You have not been about much, child. Your uncle has kept you close, so you have not had the opportunity to socialize with many young people—especially gentlemen—"

"I do know a few, Mrs. Bellweather," Candace interrupted with a laugh. "Jasper Fairgood calls every Sunday after church and Cyril Bakersfield—"

"Gammon! I am speaking of real gentlemen—not

a rustic farmer or a dressed-up popinjay. Trust me, my child, you haven't known enough men. 'Tis small wonder this Croyden makes you uncomfortable. It was the same with your mother. Poor Diana wed your father before she had been about enough to know what was what."

Candace stared at the older woman in amazement. "You knew my mother?"

"I did, indeed. Mind you, she was considerably younger than me, but I was in Town when she made her come-out, and after I married Mr. Bellweather and moved here, she used to come up to visit Emily quite often."

"But you never said a word about her—all these years, you never said a word."

Maude patted her hand and released it. "Jonathan thought it best not to talk about her, and I respected his wishes. After all, you were very young and could hardly be expected to understand what had occurred. Your uncle is a good man, Candace, but he has a blind spot about your mother. Never could forgive her for running off with her lord and leaving your father."

"Surely you do not condone what she did? It was wrong, wicked, and she left Robbie and me, too. What kind of woman would desert her children?"

Maude took her time answering. She refilled their cups and adjusted the cushion against her back before speaking again. "Diana loved you, never doubt that. I think it fair broke her heart to leave you, but she had little choice. Divorce was out of the question. Charles had found out about her affair with Lord Blackstone, and was making life miserable for everyone. He threatened to call Blackstone out."

"Why didn't he?"

The older woman shrugged her thin shoulders. "Who can say? Perhaps fear of the scandal that would have ensued, or Blackstone's expertise with a sword. I do know Jonathan advised Charles against doing anything rash, and then—then suddenly Diana was gone. It was most tragic, my dear. She was hardly older than you are now. I was thinking when you came in that you look a great deal like her."

"I wish I did not," Candace said, taking refuge behind her teacup.

"That is foolish. Your mother was a beautiful woman and a lady in every sense of the word. Her only mistake was in loving a man too much. Had she met Blackstone first, matters would have turned out very differently. Unfortunately, Diana was reared much as you have been. She had met few gentlemen when she agreed to marry Charles Stafford. I always thought it a mistake not to permit young girls a bit of freedom. Take your cousins—if Jonathan allows them a Season in Town, they will likely make fools of themselves. They should have been attending the assemblies in Heptonstall these last two years."

"We are going on Wednesday," Candace told her. "Mr. Croyden is escorting us."

"Do tell. I take it you are included in the party?"

"Yes, though I would as lief stay at home. And speaking of which, I really must leave. Mr. Croyden dines with us again this evening."

Maude chuckled. "My child, you must learn to guard your feelings more. Your dismay is writ plain for all to see. Do you loathe the prospect so much?"

"I would far rather stay here," Candace confessed, leaning down to caress the large tomcat scratching at the side of her chair.

"Then ride home and tell Jonathan I requested you bear me company this evening. Or better yet, I shall send Darby with a message—that is, if you would like to stay? I warn you I have nothing but a bit of chowder and some fresh-baked bread."

"It sounds wonderful," Candace said, "but I do not dare."

"Why ever not? Jonathan can have no objection. After all, you would be doing an old lady a kindness. You leave it to me, my dear," she said, her small eyes twinkling. "I shall take care of everything."

The clock chimed half past eight as Candace finished tidying the cozy breakfast room where she and Mrs. Bellweather had dined. Candace didn't know precisely what was in the message her hostess sent to the vicarage, but Uncle Jonathan had responded that, of course, Candace must stay if she was needed, and he would call later in the evening to escort her back to the vicarage.

Although she felt a trifle guilty for putting her uncle to so much trouble, she did not regret the evening. With a hunger she had not known she possessed, Candace had listened eagerly as Mrs. Bellweather talked about the young Diana Westhaven she had known. Memories, long repressed, came flooding back as Candace pictured her mother at seventeen, marrying the stern and very sober Charles Trent. Mrs. Bellweather blamed Charles for the tragedy as much as she did Diana, perhaps more.

"If he had been kinder to her, more understanding, Diana might never have turned to Lord Blackstone. But Charles left her alone in London for weeks at a time while he attended to his affairs at the ministry. She didn't know many people, and I suspect the first few times she allowed Julian to escort her to the theater or opera were innocent enough."

"I suppose her children were not sufficient company," Candace said, not entirely able to keep the bitterness from her voice.

Mrs. Bellweather smiled tolerantly. "The love a woman bears for her children is very different from that which she gives to a man, and quite separate from it. Diana had the nature to care passionately—and Julian awoke that in her. I saw the trouble coming, and dropped a word of warning in her ear."

"Apparently to no avail."

"No, Diana told me other ladies had their cicisbei—" She broke off at Candace's puzzled expression and explained. "I am referring to gentlemen who pay court to married women and provide escort when their husbands are too busy. 'Tis fashionable in London circles to have several such admirers. Diana claimed Lord Blackstone was no different. But, of course, he was. One had only to look at the pair of them together to see that they were deeply in love."

In love or not, what her mother did was wrong, Candace thought. She replaced the epergne in the center of the table, and gave the ornate candle holders a quick polish with her cloth. As she admired the effect, the knocker sounded, and she hurried to admit her uncle before Mrs. Bellweather could be troubled to rise from her chair in the sitting room.

Candace threw open the door, only to stare dumbly at her cousins, each clinging to one of Edward Croyden's arms, and giggling foolishly.

"Papa was going to come fetch you," Theresa said, "but Mr. Croyden volunteered instead, and, of course, we could not allow him to come alone."

"And Mama said the night was so pleasant, it would do us good to take the air," Thomasina added.

Edward Croyden merely smiled at her.

"Who is at the door?" Mrs. Bellweather called plaintively from the sitting room.

Candace stepped back, indicating the vicarage party should enter. "Come and say hello while I gather my things," she said, hoping she sounded more composed that she felt. She led the way back to the sitting room.

Mrs. Bellweather, still in her chair by the tall windows, peered at the group crowding into the small room. Her attention focused on Edward Croyden.

Candace performed the introductions, then excused herself to retrieve her gloves and hat.

Mrs. Bellweather dismissed the cousins with a curt greeting, but beckoned Croyden to come closer.

He bowed over her hand. "A pleasure to meet you, ma'am."

"I believe we may have mutual acquaintances," she said, staring at his heavy brows and thick, wavy hair. "Candace said your home is called Deerpark. May I ask precisely where it is located?"

"Somewhat north of London," he replied evasively.

She looked at him searchingly. "I knew of such

an estate once, but I believed it belonged to Lord Doncaster. Are you acquainted with him?"

"The gentleman I believe you are referring to died four years ago, but yes, I knew him very well."

Mrs. Bellweather closed her eyes briefly, then, her gnarled hands trembling, she clutched the ebony cane she kept by her chair. She struggled to her feet, accepting the arm he offered in assistance. Leaning heavily on the cane, she stared up at him. "I am most sorry to hear of his passing. He was a fine gentleman—and an honest one, which seems to be most rare these days."

Damian, gazing into her lively, intelligent eyes, nodded gravely. "Very true, ma'am, but sometimes there is just cause for a mild deception."

"An interesting viewpoint, *Mr. Croyden*, and one which I would enjoy discussing further. Perhaps you could call tomorrow—at four, shall we say?"

"I shall look forward to it," he said as Candace returned to the room.

Mrs. Bellweather smiled at her, charged Theresa and Thomasina with numerous messages for their parents, and, just as though she had known him all her life, directed Edward Croyden to retrieve Garnet from the small shed at the rear of the cottage. She cautioned him to be certain to latch the door afterward, and not to step on the cat that customarily slept by the gate.

The moon was at its fullest as the trio of young ladies stepped out of the cottage a few moments later. The pony trap, harnessed to Ruby, Garnet's stablemate, was drawn up to the door. Behind it, Edward Croyden waited with his own bay gelding and Candace's gray mare.

Thomasina took one look at the scene and turned

to her cousin. "You must be terribly tired, Candace. Would you not prefer to ride home in the trap? I would be glad to ride Garnet for you."

"Why should *you* ride Garnet?" Theresa demanded. "You do not even like to ride. If Candace is too tired, I will take Garnet home."

"May I remind you that I am the eldest and—"

"But it was my idea to come—"

Candace, aware of Edward Croyden's amusement, and embarrassed for her cousins, hushed them both. "I will ride Garnet, thank you." She strode past the trap and took the reins from Croyden.

He ordered his horse to stay and came around to give her an assist. Before she could protest, his hands encircled her waist and he lifted her easily into the saddle. When she was settled, he asked with some concern, "Are you warm enough? The night air has cooled considerably."

"I am fine, sir." In truth, she welcomed the breeze that fanned her burning cheeks, and though she wore only her light riding habit, she was far from feeling cold. She imagined she could still feel the warmth of his hands against her waist.

Theresa craned her neck around and called back, "Candace, you will not credit it, but Papa has given us all permission to drive to Heptonstall on Friday. Mr. Croyden suggested it, and besides shopping, we are to see the ruins."

"Are you?" Candace said, slanting a glance at him. Even in the moonlight his eyes seemed to taunt her. She nudged Garnet—the stupid mare seemed to want to nuzzle the gelding's neck—and replied with tolerable composure, "Your kindness exceeds all bounds, sir."

"I try to be helpful."

"And I am sure my cousins are extremely grateful."

"But it is not your cousins I wished to please. I suggested the excursion because I had the feeling you might wish to do a bit of shopping."

She looked at him sharply. He could not possibly know of her need to sell Harry's ring—but something in his voice suggested that he did.

Thomasina glanced over her shoulder. "I do not suppose you wish to come with us, Candace?"

"Watch where you are going," Theresa cried as a red fox darted across High Street just in front of the trap.

"I see him," her sister snapped, jerking the reins hard to the right.

Candace stared into the woods where the fox disappeared, wishing she could escape so easily.

"I hope you may be persuaded to join us," Croyden said, his low, melodious voice capturing her attention again. "Your aunt plans to visit several of the shops, and then we will dine at one of the inns before visiting the ruins."

Theresa's high-pitched laugh floated back to them. "La, Mr. Croyden, if you are trying to convince my cousin to accompany us, you might as well save your breath. She never goes on any excursions."

"Never?" he asked.

She dared not look at him. He undoubtedly was thinking of the picnic basket she had ordered from the Boar's Head Inn. With pretended nonchalance she said, "Theresa exaggerates—not that there are that many places to go, but we do occasionally have small outings."

"Which you attend?"

"If I am not needed at the vicarage, yes."

"Then I shall have to speak to your uncle and make sure you are not needed on Friday."

She longed to tell him she did not wish to go, but her promise to Harry weighed on her mind. Croyden was giving her the perfect excuse to visit Heptonstall. The question was, why?

Chapter 7

Damian dined at the Boar's Head Inn on Thursday evening in solitary splendor. Two overnight guests had departed that morning and, except for a couple of farmers lingering over their ale in the taproom, the place was deserted. He could have taken potluck at the Trents again, but he was wary of putting the idea in Emily's head that he was courting her daughters.

He smiled, remembering the outrageous way pretty Thomasina had flirted with him the night before. The vicar's daughter, if she ever persuaded her papa to allow her a Season in London, would give any respectable chaperon gray hair. Damian had no illusions about her. Thomasina did not consider him a possible suitor—likely she thought him too old—but she didn't mind practicing her wiles on him, and would have been pleased to count him a conquest had he shown her the slightest interest. And where Thomasina led, Theresa naturally followed.

If only Candace Stafford were so malleable, he thought. That young lady remained an enigma whose reactions were never quite what he expected. And while he admired her for her loyalty to his brother, Damian couldn't help wishing that she would trust him just a little. If she could only be brought to confide in him, he could help both her and Harry. Of course, he could always confront his brother and force him to tell the girl the truth. Damian mulled the idea over, then dismissed it. Harry would resent his interference and Candace ... Miss Candace Stafford would not think any better of him.

There must be a way, Damian thought as he finished the last bite of the lemon pie Mrs. Marley had baked that afternoon and insisted he try. He suspected the proprietress was offended that he had dined twice at the vicarage, and was determined to prove herself the better cook. She had provided a meal tasty enough to tempt any appetite, and large enough for two men. He had eaten every succulent morsel with the result that he now felt too lazy to move.

He downed the last of his ale and pushed away from the table, deciding to wait for Paddy outside. A walk in the cool night air and a cigar might help clear his mind and ease the lethargy he felt. He nodded to Phineas Marley as he passed through the taproom and stepped into the moonlit courtyard.

Paddy should be returning at any time. Damian had posted him in the woods to keep an eye on the gamekeeper's cottage during the day. Nights were no problem—no one could possibly find that hut in the velvety darkness that blanketed the woods unless they knew the way.

As he strolled across the courtyard, Damian heard the beat of hooves on High Street coming toward him at a fast clip. He paused for a moment, listening. If it were Paddy, his groom was in a fear-ful hurry.

The small Irishman came into sight seconds later, riding low over his horse's neck. When he saw Damian, he hauled on the reins and drew his lathered mount to a skittish halt.

"Two men," he gasped as he slid to the ground.

"Take it easy," Damian said, watching his groom struggle for breath.

"They're heading this way—been nosing about at the livery—asking questions about Majestic."

"Then I suggest we provide them with some answers," Damian said. He took the reins from Paddy and started walking toward the stable. "Was one of them a big redheaded fellow—arms like tree stumps?"

The groom nodded. "Kendrick—him that owns the stable—was talking to 'em when I rode in. He pointed me out, not meaning no harm. I jest told 'em how you'd seen the horse and was wishful of buying him if the owner didn't turn up."

"I take it they did not believe you?"

"Not by half, but they wasn't gonna try nothing with Kendrick there. I suspicioned they was up to no good, and spotted 'em when I left, laying for me down by the bridge. Took me for a thickwit, I guess, but I cut through the woods instead," Paddy explained, holding open the stable door.

"I don't imagine it will take them long to realize they've been duped," Damian replied, working quickly to strip the saddle and bridle off the gelding. "They're bound to come here."

Paddy, his brown eyes almost pleading, looked up at him. "I would've faced 'em, gov, if an' it were a fair fight. I didn't run because I was scared."

Damian glanced at him, then nodded. "I never thought so, Paddy. Only a fool would have ridden into a trap. We shall see how eager these lads are to talk to us when the odds are more even. I propose we wait for them in the taproom."

He led the way to the inn, unaware that Paddy had to walk double-time to keep up with his long strides. Anger burned inside Damian for the sort of men who would lay an ambush, especially when they outnumbered their prey. He was nearly certain this pair was responsible for shooting Harry as well, and that was a score he intended to settle— once he found out who had hired them.

Damian had a word with Phineas Marley, then carried two tankards of ale to a table facing the door. He and Paddy settled in their chairs, but there was nothing relaxed about either man. Damian kept his gaze on the door.

The redhead called Turk strode in first and stopped abruptly when he saw them sitting at the table. His partner, hard on his heels, stumbled into him. "What the—"

Turk flung an arm out to shut him up, then walked slowly toward Damian. The redhead stood over six foot tall, and muscles bulged in his huge arms. Just looking at him was sufficient to intimidate most men. His mouth formed a parody of a grin. "Well, if it ain't the dandy that sent us on a wild-goose chase and that little bitsy fellow that skittered off in the woods. I'd say this was our lucky day, Fred."

"Your mistake, my friend," Damian said coolly as he rose to his feet. "I allowed you to walk out of here once—you should not have come back."

The redhead involuntarily stepped back a pace.

He outweighed Damian by thirty pounds and topped his height by an inch, but he didn't see the slightest trace of fear in the dark, smoky eyes challenging him.

The younger man with the grizzly beard glanced around furtively. The innkeeper and a couple of yokels were watching from the corner of the bar. They'd get no help from that quarter. He slowly reached beneath his coat for his pistol.

"I wouldn't try it," Paddy said, his own pistol aimed directly at the fellow's heart. "Not unless you was wishful of making this your last day."

"What's your interest in this?" Turk blustered. We're only trying to find a rat that cheated at cards. You got no call to interfere, unless—his bleeding lordship didn't hire you, too, did he?"

Damian smiled, but it never touched his eyes. "The rat you refer to so glibly is my brother. I resent the aspersions you have cast on his character."

"Huh?" Fred said, his eyes darting from Paddy to Damian.

"Should I elucidate? You ambushed my brother, wounding him in the shoulder, then chased him halfway across England. It is fortunate for you that he lives. What I want to know, gentlemen, is the name of the lord who was foolish enough to employ you." As he spoke, Damian removed his coat and draped it across the back of his chair. Then he carefully rolled up the sleeves of his linen shirt.

"Bugger you," Turk growled. "I ain't listening to this pap." He turned to leave, but Damian's hand gripped his shoulder and forced him to turn around. A lightning right to the jaw landed before Turk could lift a hand, and a second later the redhead lay sprawled on the floor.

102

Paddy cocked his pistol and waved it at Fred. "Back away and keep out of this, or my finger's likely to slip."

At the bar the innkeeper and the farmers laid their bets.

Turk fingered his jaw, his eyes narrowing as he appraised Damian. "Mighty big talk when you got your man holding a gun on us."

"Paddy won't interfere—as long as the fight's fair. Get up."

Turk rose unsteadily to his feet. After stripping off his coat, he circled the table warily. He feinted twice, hoping to get his opponent to lower his guard. Damian watched the man's eyes and was ready when the redhead threw a punch. He blocked it with his arm, jabbed a quick left, then a right, to Turk's stomach.

The big man backed off, shaking his head. He wasn't used to fighting fair, and he knew he was in trouble. But he had an edge. He managed to get a fist in over Damian's guard, knowing he was leaving his own chest unprotected. A strong right knocked the wind from him, and he doubled over. His hand snaked to his boot and came up with a knife.

The blade glistened in the candlelight as he raised his arm to throw the dagger.

Paddy fired in the same instant, the sound of the pistol shot deafening in the small room.

The knife clattered to the floor, and Turk howled, holding his wounded hand to his chest, the blood rapidly staining his dingy shirt.

Damian gazed at him dispassionately, then glanced at Paddy. "I do wish you had not done that."

"He pulled a shiv, gov. Couldn't let him knife you, now, could I?"

Fred, whose swarthy coloring had lightened a shade or two, backed uneasily toward the door. He stumbled into Phineas Marley, who shoved him back into the room. "I don't think the gentleman is through with his questions."

"I need a doctor," Turk muttered, collapsing onto a chair.

"I shall see you get the same excellent care you gave my brother," Damian said. He took his time rolling down his sleeves, then slipped on his coat. When he had adjusted it to his satisfaction, he glanced at the innkeeper. "Have you an old rag or something to wrap around his hand?"

Phineas nodded and pulled a soiled napkin from his apron. He tossed it on the table in front of the redhead.

"You can't keep me here—'tis murder. There's witnesses," Turk threatened, nodding toward the farmers.

"Do you think so? I rather believe these gentlemen will testify that you drew your knife with the intent to kill me. The more I think of it, the world would be better off without you."

As the farmers nodded in agreement, Turk sent an imploring look to his partner.

"Do not expect help from that direction," Damian warned. "His sort is ineffective unless he's shooting from ambush. Is that not right, Fred?"

"I ain't shot nobody," the grizzly bearded younger man protested. "It was Turk what shot your brother—"

"Shut up, you bleeding sot," Turk warned.

Fred shrugged. "Look, we was only doing what

104

his lordship told us. He said as 'ow your brother cheated him—"

"He lied," Damian interrupted quietly, but with such conviction, no one in the room could doubt him. "I want his name."

The two exchanged looks. Turk, his eyes full of cunning, glanced up at Damian. "I ain't about to die to protect some bleeding toff. You get me a doctor and see to my hand, and I'll give you his lordship's name."

"Unfortunately, you are not in a position to bargain," Damian said. He strolled casually to the fireplace and picked up a poker. "I understand an effective treatment for a wound is to cauterize it with fire."

"You wouldn't," Turk said, sweat beading on his forehead.

"I would indeed. I am very fond of my brother, you see," Damian replied, holding the poker over the flames. No one in the room moved or spoke. After a moment he removed the poker. Holding the glowing red end in front of him, he walked toward Turk.

"The name?"

"Cardiff," the redhead spat out, cringing back in his chair. "The Duke of Cardiff."

After Turk and Fred were allowed to leave, the farmers stood to a drink, and Phineas compensated for the one broken chair, Damian sat and watched his groom clean and reload his pistol. Paddy seemed in excessively high spirits.

He looked up to catch Damian's gaze on him and grinned widely. "Guess we showed 'em, gov."

"We did, indeed, but I sincerely hope you are not planning to shoot anyone else."

"Jest staying prepared in case that Turk fellow comes sneaking back."

"I believe we have likely seen the last of that pair."

"You think they'll go to London and tell the duke what happened?"

Damian considered the matter as he drained the last of his ale. "I rather doubt it. They bungled the affair from start to finish, and Cardiff will not be pleased. If Turk has any sense at all, he'll put as much distance as possible between himself and His Grace."

Paddy laid the pistol aside and smiled happily. "Then tomorrow I can tell Master Harry 'tis safe to come out?"

"Not yet."

"But, gov, if we've seen the back of those thugs—"

"There is still Cardiff," Damian reminded him. "His greed has placed him in an impossible position. If Harry lives to refute the vowel Cardiff doctored, the duke is finished in England. The scandal will ruin him. I imagine he is growing extremely concerned that he has not received word from his hirelings."

"You think he'll come here?"

Damian shrugged. "If Turk communicated with him, I would bet on it. He cannot afford to allow Harry to live."

"Blimey, I hadn't thought of that."

"I have thought of little else, but do not let it concern you. I rather suspect we have a few days' grace. Now, tomorrow, I want you to return to Deerpark—"

"And leave you here alone?" the groom interrupted. "Not on your life. Why, jest think what might have happened if I hadn't been here tonight."

"Paddy," Damian said quietly, leveling a look at him that warned the groom not to argue. "I will be perfectly safe for a few days, but my mother must be desperately worried. First Harry disappears, and then we vanish—you must go back. I will give you a letter for her, and I shall also require additional clothing. Have Phipps pack a few things for me."

The groom nodded morosely.

Taking pity on him, Damian smiled. "Cheer up. You may tell the countess that I expect you to return with all possible speed."

As they discussed the details of the journey, one of the farmers rose and approached the table. He coughed discreetly, and when Damian glanced up, said, "Forgive me for intruding, Mr. Croyden, but I could not leave without telling you how much I admired the manner in which you dispatched those ruffians. While I generally do not approve of fisticuffs, and would not be so presumptuous as to inquire into the nature of your quarrel, it must be apparent to the most unobservant eye that those men were not the sort we wish to see in our neighborhood."

"If your remarks are intended as a compliment, thank you, sir. You are?"

"I beg your pardon. In the excitement of that fracas I quite forgot that we had not been introduced. My name, sir, is Jasper Fairgood."

So this was Candace's suitor. Damian looked at the young man more closely. Despite his ponderous manner, he appeared no more than thirty, though his sandy hair was already receding above a wide forehead, sparse brows, and pale blue eyes.

"I have heard of you, Mr. Fairgood," Damian said. He spared a glance at Paddy, the sort of unspoken communication that frequently passed between them, and his groom immediately murmured an excuse and left the room. Gesturing toward the empty chair, Damian added, "Will you join me for a few moments? I believe we have a mutual acquaintance."

"Now, that, sir, is most surprising. I have not been in London for some years, and cannot imagine who would be kind enough to bring my name to your attention." He pulled out his pocket watch and checked the time, indecision plainly showing in his eyes.

"The Trents mentioned your name when I dined at the vicarage last evening."

Jasper stared at him, then, realizing his rudeness, shook his head. "You must forgive my astonishment, Mr. Croyden, but the Reverend Mr. Trent entertains so rarely—are you, perhaps, an old friend?"

"We met but recently," Damian told him, then gestured to Marley to bring more ale. "A delightful family, but, of course, you know that. I understand your acquaintance is of long standing?"

"Indeed, yes," Jasper said as he took his seat. "My family was one of the first to welcome the Trents when they settled here some twenty years ago. I should tell you that I have a tidy little property north of the village that the Fairgoods have farmed for the past hundred years. I fancy that I am the first, however, to employ new agricultural techniques, and to expand our boundaries. May I ask if you own any land, Mr. Croyden?"

"A modest estate," Damian said, thinking how amused his stepmother would be to hear the vast acreage that comprised Deerpark described in such a manner.

Jasper nodded approvingly. "I suspected as much. I find there is a discernable difference between men who own their property and those who are mere tenant farmers. I suppose that it is because we, as owners, must bear the full burden of responsibility. Do you not find it so?"

"I hadn't given the matter much thought—"

"Few men have," Jasper interrupted. "I mentioned the idea to the Reverend Mr. Trent, who is naturally a very learned gentleman, and you may imagine my astonishment when I discovered he had never considered the notion. Have you had much conversation with him?"

"A little."

"Ah, I gather you found him difficult to converse with. I, too, sir. One would think, isolated as we are, that he would welcome the opportunity to speak with another who, if I may be pardoned for saying so, has obtained no small degree of learning. However, on the few occasions I have been privileged to dine at the vicarage, the good reverend retires immediately after dinner to labor over his sermon, and one does not see him again for the rest of the evening."

Damian's opinion of the good reverend rose another notch.

"A less perceptive gentleman might have his sensibilities wounded by such behavior," Jasper continued. "But having known the Trents for so many years, I am aware of the reverend's little eccentricities and, of course, make allowances. I hope you did not take offense when you dined there? I can assure you none was intended. And, of course, the ladies quite make up for any lack of warmth on the reverend's part."

"I did find the ladies charming," Damian managed to say when Jasper paused to take a drink of ale. "As a means of repaying their hospitality, I am escorting them on an excursion to Heptonstall tomorrow."

"Indeed? I am surprised that you would be allowed—not that you are not in every way an estimable gentleman—but the reverend seldom permits his daughters to go beyond the confines of Thatchwood. Heptonstall, you say? Well, I am certain Thomasina and Theresa will enjoy such an expedition tremendously. Does Mrs. Trent accompany you?"

"She does, and Miss Stafford also."

Jasper opened his mouth, then shut it, for once left speechless. He recovered quickly, however, and shook his head. "I am certain you misunderstood, Mr. Croyden. Miss Stafford does not indulge in anything in the nature of a frivolous pursuit. She is far too busy assisting her uncle in the affairs of the parish. Her cousins may get up a picnic, or go for a jaunt to visit historic ruins or such, but not she. It is one of the things I most admire about her."

"Understandably, but I believe she is making an exception tomorrow. Perhaps because of the assembly—you know how the ladies are, always needing new ribbons for their gowns, or new gloves," Damian said, and derived considerable satisfaction when Fairgood merely stared at him. The man's confidence that Damian was mistaken had annoyed him out of reason.

"Assembly?"

"Oh, have you not heard?" Damian asked innocently. "I am taking a small party—just the ladies from the vicarage and one or two others—to the Heptonstall Assembly Rooms on Wednesday. Mrs. Trent is making the arrangements. Of course, I could be mistaken, but I thought she mentioned your name. . . ."

"She may have tried to reach me, but I have been away for the past week," Jasper said, for the first time that evening looking uncertain.

"I am certain she did."

"Yes, that must be it. Still, I am puzzled that Candace—Miss Stafford—would agree to such a scheme without discussing it with me first," he said, and with the air of one imparting a grave confidence, added, "We have an understanding between us."

"You are affianced? I did not realize—"

"Oh, not officially," Jasper hastened to explain. "But 'tis common knowledge in the village."

"I see," Damian murmured, but he could not imagine Candace with this dour and somber young farmer. He had a sudden urge to observe the pair of them together and suggested, "Perhaps you would care to join us in the morning? We leave from the vicarage at half past nine."

Chapter 8

Impossible, thought Candace, watching the chaotic scene in the vicarage drive from her bedchamber window. She had known it would be difficult to elude her cousins and Edward Croyden long enough to sell Harry's ring, but she had believed it might be managed if she were careful. But now it looked as though half of Thatchwood intended to visit Heptonstall.

She spotted Edward Croyden's tall figure, standing near the carriage he had rented from the livery, and glared at him. She didn't know how, or why, or what nefarious purpose he had in mind, but she felt certain he had invited Jasper Fairgood to join the party only to vex her. And if that was his intent, it was succeeding remarkably well.

"Candace?" Theresa called from the stairs. "Mama sent me to see what is keeping you. Everyone is ready to leave."

"I am coming," she replied, and picked up her reticule. Harry's ring, wrapped securely in her handkerchief, was tucked neatly inside the beaded bag, along with a delicate string of pearls. The necklace, given to her on her sixteenth birthday, had belonged to her mother. For two years it had lain at the bottom of her wardrobe in its long velvet box. Candace could not bring herself to wear it, or allow Thomasina to. Her cousin openly coveted the necklace, and frequently warned her that the pearls would lose their luster if they weren't worn.

"Candace! Do come—oh, there you are," Theresa said as her cousin stepped into the hall. "Mrs. Fairgood is starting to lecture us on punctuality. Why did Jasper have to bring his mother along?"

"I suggest you ask Mr. Croyden. He probably invited her."

"Well, if he did, I am sure he is regretting it now. He told her that while punctuality may be accounted a virtue in the country, no one in London who has the least pretensions to being fashionable would dream of arriving on time."

"Did she tell him that her cousin, the baron, would never keep a lady waiting?"

Theresa giggled. "I believe she was starting to do so when Mama sent me after you."

"Hush now," Candace warned as they stepped outside. Despite her problems, a surge of anticipation lifted her spirits as she felt the warmth of the sun, and noticed the nearly cloudless blue sky. The circular sweep of freshly cut lawn opposite the drive was still damp with dew and sparkled with a lush greenness. Tomorrow, the pesky dandelions would return, but today it looked perfect and smelled wonderfully. It was the sort of morning one accepted as a gift.

Candace inhaled deeply, glad that she had chosen a simple white muslin walking dress with a light pelisse that could be discarded if the day turned exceptionally warm. Her wrap was trimmed with the same Pamona green ribbons that adorned her straw bonnet, and tied securely beneath her chin. She adjusted the ribbons and surveyed the scene before her from beneath its wide brim.

Aunt Emily and Thomasina were already seated in Edward Croyden's carriage at the head of the drive. It was a large and cumbersome vehicle, the bright yellow paint faded and chipped, but the best the livery had to offer. Michael Kendrick, the owner's eldest boy, was on the box, handling the reins of two powerful-looking geldings.

Behind him, in the ancient black coach that Jasper drove to church on Sundays, Maria Fairgood waited impatiently, the feathers on her black high-crowned bonnet waving in the light breeze. And at the end of the drive, Cyril Bakersfield, already mounted on a handsome black stallion, broke off his conversation with Jasper and Edward Croyden to gaze adoringly at Theresa.

The other gentlemen stepped forward to greet the young ladies. Jasper offered his arm to Candace. "Good morning, my dear. I was just telling Mr. Croyden that, naturally, you will wish to ride with Mother and me. She was saying only yesterday that she has not seen you in some time, and, of course, I am eager to tell you about my visit to Mr. Coke in Norfolk. Believe that I do not understate the matter when I tell you that Holkham greatly exceeded my every expectation. Indeed, I am eager to experiment with some of the tilling methods Mr. Coke recommended."

"How fascinating," Croyden said dryly.

Candace, aware of his smoky eyes silently inviting her to share his amusement, struggled to ignore him. She turned to Jasper, managing a smile for his benefit, and laid her hand on his sleeve. "It *is* fascinating, and I am glad you found the visit

114

worthwhile, but perhaps we should not keep your mother waiting."

Croyden, unprincipled rogue that he was, had the audacity to grin at Theresa. "Come along, little one. I cannot promise you so enlightening a journey as Mr. Fairgood will provide, but I shall tell you about Almack's if you like."

At the mention of the famous assembly rooms in London, Theresa stared up at Croyden, unable to tell if he was jesting. "Have you really been in Almack's?"

He bent his head close to hers as though imparting some great secret, and murmured, "My aunt's brother-in-law on my mother's side is a cousin, twice removed, of Lady Sefton's, and she, as you undoubtedly know, is one of the patronesses."

Theresa giggled. "I do not believe you, sir."

"And neither do I," muttered Candace, watching them walk off together.

"I beg your pardon?" Jasper said, but his attention was distracted as his mother poked her head out the carriage window and called to him.

"Jasper! I am waiting."

"Yes, Mother," he replied with the ingrained habit of years of obedience.

Heptonstall was reached by climbing a steep grade. The original inhabitants had chosen the high terrace overlooking the valley because the approaches could be readily controlled and, if necessary, defended, and where, despite the high altitude, wheat and oats could still be grown on the edges of the moorland. By London standards, it could hardly be called a town, but to those who lived in the small surrounding villages like Thatchwood, it seemed a thriving metropolis.

The ruins of the old church tower were visible as they approached, and Jasper pointed out that the lower masonry dated back to the thirteenth century.

Candace nodded while silently wishing he would spend less time pointing out landmarks with which she was already familiar, and set his horses to a faster pace. It had taken them two very long hours to reach Heptonstall. However, she knew it would be useless to suggest such a thing, even though Croyden's carriage had long since disappeared over the crest of the hill. Mrs. Fairgood would only say that patience provides its own reward, a maxim Candace had never quite understood, but which the older woman quoted often on the authority of her cousin, the baron.

"Candace, Mother asked you a question," Jasper said, a hint of reproach in his voice.

"I am sorry—I was admiring the valley below us. It is rather beautiful, is it not?"

Maria Fairgood was not to be placated. "Daydreaming is a waste of time, and you will do well, my dear, to rid yourself of the habit. I find it most annoying to have to repeat myself."

Candace refused to apologize again. She sat with her hands neatly folded and gazed attentively at Mrs. Fairgood.

Jasper, ever the peacemaker between the two, intervened. "Mother was asking how you came to meet Mr. Croyden."

"Uncle Jonathan invited him to dine with us after meeting him at the church. I believe they attended the same college."

"Humph. Hardly a recommendation. What is he doing in Thatchwood, may I ask?" Her full, colorless lips settled into a frown, and she peered at Candace as though she were responsible for Croyden's presence.

"As I understand it, he is interested in buying the hall."

"What? Why, that is preposterous. Squire Epsom would never sell—the land has been in his family for seven generations. I cannot believe such a thing."

"Perhaps you should ask Mr. Croyden yourself," Candace suggested sweetly.

"I certainly shall," Maria declared. "My instincts are seldom at fault, and I tell you frankly that I mistrust the man. Buy the hall, indeed! Giving himself airs, if you ask me. Trying to insinuate himself in our good graces. Both of you will do well to follow my lead and have as little to do with the gentleman as possible."

"Difficult, do you not think, since we *are* his guests," Candace said, lifting her chin a bit. It was irrational of her to argue. She should feel delighted that Mrs. Fairgood thought Edward Croyden an impostor, not resentful.

"The situation is unfortunate," Maria said. "If Jasper had sought my counsel before agreeing to this excursion, I certainly should have advised against it. However, what's done is done. We must simply keep our distance."

With Jasper driving, that would not be hard, Candace thought as they finally turned on Market Street. She spotted the faded yellow carriage drawn to the side of the wide, cobblestoned street and the rest of their party standing nearby. As they

117

drew near, she could hear Theresa's high-pitched giggles and Aunt Emily's softer laughter. At least someone was enjoying the morning.

When Jasper brought his team to a halt, Edward Croyden strode to the side of the carriage and lifted a hand to assist Candace to alight. "Did you enjoy the drive? Are you ready for something to eat, or would you prefer to stroll a bit first?"

Nothing in his tone or his words betrayed his amusement, but Candace knew he was laughing at her. When he was angry or annoyed, his dark eyes appeared almost black—and cold as a night on the moors. But when he was amused, his eyes seemed a warm brown, and invited one to join the jest.

She accepted his arm as she descended but avoided his gaze as she replied, "Whatever the others wish will be agreeable to me."

"Well, I am starving," Theresa declared. "We have been waiting for you for ages. What took you so long?"

Maria Fairgood stepped down from the carriage, assisted by her son, and stared disapprovingly at Theresa. "*We* traveled at a moderate pace entirely suitable to the occasion. Jasper would never think of racing his cattle when there are ladies aboard his carriage—no gentleman of breeding would."

"Someone should tell that to Lord Drayton," Croyden murmured, but only loud enough for Candace to hear.

She glanced up at him curiously. "Do you know Lord Drayton?"

"Everyone in England knows Madcap Johnny. The latest *on dit* is that he broke the record for driving from London to Bath, and that his new wife was with him at the time."

Thomasina moved closer to Croyden and fluttered her lashes as she looked up at him. "I have heard Lady Drayton is quite beautiful. Have you seen her, sir?"

Croyden grinned. "I have, and no, little one, she is not as pretty as you."

Not at all abashed, Thomasina basked in his praise. "Oh, I wish we were in London now."

"Well, I do not see what is so grand about Town life," Cyril Bakersfield said as he came up to them with Mrs. Trent on one arm and Theresa on the other.

"But I thought you enjoyed it," Theresa said, referring to his sojourn in London the year before.

He shrugged. "I believe it well enough for a visit, but frightfully expensive. Did you not find it so, sir?"

Croyden, whose monthly income was probably treble what young Bakersfield received, nodded gravely. "I avoid London as much as possible."

Annoyed at the deference the others accorded Mr. Croyden, Maria snapped, "That is understandable, sir. To appreciate London, one must have the proper entrée into polite Society. My cousin, the baron, opens his town house every fall. I have visited him there on numerous occasions and thoroughly enjoyed the experience."

Emily Trent looked nervously from one to the other. She disliked scenes of any sort and suggested tactfully, "Perhaps we should visit some of the shops before we eat. I believe I saw some very pretty ribbons displayed in the window at the end of the street."

Maria, perversely, announced she intended to inspect the kerseymere displayed at the blackened stone house directly across from them. Thomasina and Theresa voted to accompany their mother, and Cyril would inevitably go wherever Theresa chose. Jasper looked at Candace expectantly.

"Do go with your mother, and I will join you directly," she said, then turned to her aunt. "The clasp on Mama's pearls has come loose. If you will allow me, I should like to inquire at the goldsmith's to see if it can be mended."

"Alone? My dear, I cannot think that would be wise," Emily fretted. "I know you are accustomed to going about unescorted, but this is not like Thatchwood, where one knows everyone."

"If you will permit me, Mrs. Trent, I shall escort Miss Stafford, and then we may all meet at the White Lion," Croyden offered, and consulted his pocket watch. "It is half past eleven. Shall we say in an hour's time?"

Mrs. Fairgood sniffed audibly, and said to Emily, "You must do as you think best, of course, but I certainly would not allow a young lady in my charge to go off with a gentleman unchaperoned."

"Oh, for heaven's sakes, Maria," Emily retorted, surprising them all. "This is not London, and Mr. Croyden enjoys my husband's complete trust—and mine."

Jasper looked extremely vexed, but his mother was already offended and he dared not offer to go with Candace instead. Thomasina suddenly remembered a desire to purchase a small clasp for her blue cottage cloak, and suggested she go with her cousin, though it was Edward Croyden her gaze lingered on.

"You will come with me, young lady," Emily said, and pinched her elder daughter's arm.

Candace remained quiet, unable to think of any way to refuse Croyden's escort. To do so would create a fuss, and though that would please Mrs. Fairgood, Aunt Emily would be terribly embarrassed, especially after her staunch defense of him. Reluctantly, Candace accepted his arm as the various parties separated, and strolled with him toward the north end of Market Street.

She kept her gaze straight ahead, oblivious of the vendors hawking their wares from the tall windows and open doorways of the solid stone houses. Though her arm rested but lightly on Croyden's sleeve, she imagined she could feel heat rising from beneath his coat and the sensation made her blind to all else. They walked in silence for several moments until Candace felt compelled to say something. Anything.

"We are most fortunate the day is so fine," she remarked finally.

"We are, indeed."

She glanced up quickly, catching the betraying liveliness of his eyes. He was laughing at her again.

"And 'tis likely the afternoon will turn uncomfortably warm. May we now dispense with the weather? I would far rather you rail at me than make polite conversation."

Despite herself, her lips twitched. "You make polite conversation exceedingly difficult, Mr. Croyden. What do you suggest we discuss?"

"Tell me about your mother."

"Mama?" she asked, startled.

"You said she left you a strand of pearls, from which I deduce, she died. When?"

The question may have been abrupt, but his

voice was warmly sympathetic. Candace's free hand toyed with the ribbons of her bonnet. Except with Mrs. Bellweather, she had never talked about her mother. Stalling for time, she said, "That would certainly not be considered within the realm of polite conversation. Why do you wish to know?"

"Because I suspect you are still grieving for her," he replied gently. "You never speak of her. I felt much the same when my mother died. I think we might have more in common than you believe."

"I am sure the . . . the circumstances were different."

"Perhaps not. They both abandoned us—I can still remember how that feels, though I was only four at the time."

They had reached the goldsmith's, and Candace halted in front of the door. She looked up at him and replied with unwonted frankness, "My mother abandoned me *before* she died. She eloped to Paris with a member of the aristocracy, and after he was killed in a duel, she shot herself. I was eight years old at the time. Do you still think we have much in common?"

Suppressing a strong impulse to sweep her into his arms and kiss away the hurt reflected in her green eyes, he sought for words to comfort her. But what could he say? What could anyone say?

Candace did not wait for a reply. Lifting her chin proudly, she said, "Now, if you will excuse me, I have private business to transact and I would prefer to do so alone." She expected him to protest, but he merely nodded and withdrew a cigar.

"I'll wait for you out here."

Damian, leaning against the wall of the goldsmith's shop, blew a cloud of smoke and contemplated the situation. He wished again that Candace would trust him enough to allow him to help her, instead of forcing him to do so by rather devious methods.

Early yesterday he had ridden to Heptonstall and had a word with Silas Crandle, the proprietor of Crandle & Bailey, Goldsmiths and Diamond Merchants. The gentleman had been effusively helpful once Damian had given him a draft on his bank. Crandle would buy Harry's ring from Candace, and then hold it for Damian. He could not let the ring go out of the family, no matter how much Harry wished to assert his independence.

Earlier, Damian had toyed with the notion of entering the shop with Candace, just to see what she would do next. The pearls had been a plausible excuse, and he had thought it might be amusing to see what ingenious pretext she would find to rid herself of his company. Only, he had not expected the revelation about her mother. The haunted look in her eyes had made him feel like a scoundrel for tormenting her.

Candace stepped out the door as he was trying to think of a way to restore her spirits. Her brave smile, barely tugging at the corner of her lips, made him feel worse.

"Thank you for waiting, Mr. Croyden. We can join the others now."

He consulted his watch again. "We still have half an hour, and there are a few purchases I would like to make here, if you would not mind coming in again with me?"

"Oh, I had not thought—but, of course I will, if you wish."

"I do," he said, taking her arm and turning her

123

around. "I need your advice. Your aunt has been exceedingly kind to me, and I would like to buy her a small gift to express my appreciation. What do you suggest?"

"I suggest we find another shop. Crandle & Bailey's is quite expensive."

"And I am quite wealthy," he informed her as he opened the door and ushered her in. "Help me choose something she would like, and you are not to inquire the price."

Mr. Crandle hurried over to assist them, but Damian waved him away. "We shall just look about a bit, and call you when we need your assistance."

Candace glanced around in helpless confusion. Besides the splendid array of necklaces, bracelets, and rings, there were elaborately decorated fans, jewel-encrusted traveling cases for a lady's cosmetics, tiny figures of fine porcelain, beautifully worked cameos, and jeweled clasps of all sorts.

"What do you think of this?" Damian asked her, picking up one of the exquisite tiny cameos designed to be worn as a pendant.

Candace shook her head. "It is much too dear. I cannot think Aunt Emily would be comfortable accepting such a gift from a virtual stranger."

"I, my dear girl, am hardly a stranger. Your uncle has allowed me to run tame in his house. Surely that elevates me to the status of old and valued family friend."

"Even if you *were* an old and valued friend, a point which I do not concede, the cameo would still be unacceptable."

"A gold cross, then? What could be more appropriate for the wife of a vicar?"

Candace laughed. "Have you never bought a lady

a gift, Mr. Croyden? The rules dictate candy, flowers, and books."

"Rules were made to be broken," he said, absurdly pleased that he had made her laugh. "Besides, I gave my aunt Hattie a cross, and she was very well pleased."

"But she is related to you."

"According to the Book of Genesis, we are all sons and daughters of Adam and Eve, so somewhere along the line we must be related. Now, be a good girl and help me pick out a gift, or I shall tell your uncle you dispute the Bible."

"A Bible would make a very nice gift."

"Perhaps, but I feel certain your uncle has sufficient Bibles in the house. It shall be the cross," he declared, and motioned to Crandle to wrap it up. "Now, Thomasina mentioned she wanted a clasp—what color is her cloak?"

"Blue, but you must not—"

"Hush. Your cousins are like sisters to me, and you cannot tell me it is unsuitable to give my sister a clasp."

"Apparently, I cannot tell you anything."

"You are learning." He picked up a small blue and gold clasp. The top was exquisitely cut tourmaline that caught and reflected the light. "Will this match her cloak?"

She watched helplessly as he selected his gifts and had Crandle wrap them. For Theresa, whose cloak was green, he selected an emerald clasp that anyone could see was far too expensive. But when she protested, he told her brazenly that it was mere paste, causing poor Mr. Crandle to suffer a fit of coughing.

For her uncle he selected a Staffordshire pearlware figure of Saint Paul preaching at Athens. About ten inches tall, the gray-bearded figure stood barefoot next to a tan pedestal supporting a quill and a scroll. The whole was mounted on a black marbleized base.

"It will look splendid on his desk, do you not think?"

She nodded, touched by his thoughtfulness. The gift was perfect, and she knew her uncle would treasure it.

"Now, go wait by the door while I select something for you."

"I do not want—"

"Must you be so argumentative? Go, or I shall have to find Mrs. Fairgood and ask her advice." She laughed, but obediently walked toward the door. When she was out of earshot, he motioned to Crandle and quietly told him what he wished.

Knowing Candace would not accept any jewelry from him, he had watched to see which items she had admired. Her taste was excellent. She had lingered over a Derby figure of a tiny shepherdess wearing a white hat with a rose ribbon, a rose-laced bodice with a gilt-edged white skirt decorated with floral sprays, and a white flower-filled apron. The latter she held out with her right hand, and in her left she carried a tiny nosegay of roses. The detail was exceptional.

When it was wrapped and added to the rest of his purchases, Damian joined her at the door. "I bought you flowers," he said. "Quite unexceptional."

"You are incorrigible, Mr. Croyden. Crandle & Bailey do not sell flowers."

"Do they not? Then I have been duped."

She shook her head in mock despair as they left

the shop. There was no point in arguing with him. Whatever he had purchased, she would return with a polite note. She was about to offer to carry one of the bundles, when she heard the church bells chiming. "Good heavens, I had no idea we were so long. We shall be late, and I shudder to think what Mrs. Fairgood will have to say. Perhaps you should have bought her a gift as well."

Damian chuckled. "Do you think a diamond clasp would endear me to her?"

"Not in the least. You would only make her thoroughly miserable. Her acquisitive nature would yearn to accept it, but her pride would not allow her to."

"You almost tempt me to go back to Crandle's."

"We haven't time," Candace said. "And I hope you will forget I said such a thing. It was uncharitable of me, and probably quite undeserved."

"But I was vastly relieved to hear you say it," he told her as they approached the White Lion.

Curious, she glanced up at him. "Dare I ask why?"

"I was beginning to think you were a saint."

She laughed then. "Far from it, Mr. Croyden."

He opened the door just as Jasper Fairgood was about to step out. The young man halted abruptly and looked suspiciously from one to the other.

"Mother and Mrs. Trent sent me to find you, Candace. Do you not realize the time? We were growing worried."

"I am sorry, Jasper. Mr. Croyden had numerous purchases to make. Are the others here?"

"We have all been here for some time," he said reprovingly. "And you know how much value Mother places on punctuality."

"I will apologize," she murmured in a subdued voice.

Damian saw the way the laughter left her face, and how her eyes turned gray again. Annoyed, he gestured for Fairgood to lead the way. What the devil was the matter with the man? He was the sort that, had he been around when fire was invented, would have rushed to douse it with water. Candace deserved better.

Mrs. Fairgood, insulted at being kept waiting, greeted their arrival tartly. Though Candace apologized, the older woman was in no mood to be appeased and insisted on delivering a lengthy homily on the virtues of promptness.

Damian endured it as long as possible, then signaled to the waiter to begin serving. He smiled at Mrs. Fairgood. "I quite agree, madam. Nothing can stigmatize a lady as being ill bred so readily as habitual tardiness . . . unless, of course, it is that she lacks the ability to set those about her at ease. That quality alone, according to *London Etiquette*, defines a true lady. 'Tis a most interesting book. If you have not seen a copy, I should be glad to send you one."

After a gasp of astonishment, Mrs. Fairgood inhaled deeply, her considerable bosom expanding an inch, and stated firmly, "I do not require a book to instruct me on the precepts of being a lady, Mr. Croyden."

"Certainly not. Everyone knows that some things cannot be learned from a mere book. Mrs. Trent is a perfect example," he said, smiling at the lady seated at the opposite end of the table. "I am quite certain she has not learned her excellent manners by reading about them—they come to her quite naturally. And by the example she sets, she teaches her daughters and her niece, who, I fear, will likely receive a scold this evening for her tardiness, though the fault was entirely mine."

"I am surprised you own to any faults," Mrs. Fairgood sniffed.

"Oh, I have dozens, as I am sure must any gentleman who remains a bachelor," he said with an easy laugh. "I believe it takes a wife to truly civilize a man. Do you not think so, Mr. Fairgood?"

"I am not certain what you mean," Jasper said. He'd been embarrassed when his mother took Candace to task, though he knew her intention was only to instruct the young lady who would one day be her daughter-in-law. She had often said that Candace, lacking a mother to teach her the finer points of conduct, would find herself at a disadvantage in London unless someone took her in hand. Still, he wished his mother had not chosen to admonish Candace in public, and in front of Edward Croyden, of all people.

"I believe I know what you mean," Emily Trent said, thankful for the opportunity to turn the conversation. "If it were left to my husband, no calling cards would ever be returned, no dinners ever arranged, or notes of regret sent."

"Precisely. In London, it is the lady of the house who tends to such matters. . . ."

Candace sat quietly, listening as the talk flowed around her. She knew Mr. Croyden had deliberately intervened to spare her a lecture, and while she was thankful, she wondered at his background. As he discussed the finer points of protocol required of anyone hopeful for a successful London Season, she realized how conversant he was. Only a gentleman who traveled in the first circle of Society could describe the interior of Almack's so completely, or have such intimate knowledge of that exclusive gentleman's club known as White's.

Even Mrs. Fairgood was silenced for once as Croyden regaled them with tales of the Prince Regent and the Carleton House set, and luncheon passed almost pleasantly, though as they were leaving, she did remark that the fish had an odd taste, and the sweetbreads were not sufficiently cooked.

The rest of the party had no complaints, and were in high spirits. "What now?" Thomasina asked Mr. Croyden as they stepped outside. "Shall we visit the church tower?"

"Whatever you wish," he replied. "But perhaps we should stop at the assembly rooms first, and enter our names in the subscription book. Then we can continue on to the ruins, and from there drive back to Thatchwood."

Mrs. Fairgood decided to wait in the carriage. She had no interest in the assembly rooms at Heptonstall, remarking that they must surely suffer in comparison to those of Bath and Harrogate. Consequently, she was the only one to notice the two elderly ladies who turned and stared after Edward Croyden as he shepherded his party into the brick building at Market and Center streets.

"I am certain it was him," the elder of the two commented as they passed by. "But I wonder what brings him here."

"And who was the young lady with him?" the other demanded, looking back over her shoulder.

Chapter 9

Sitting in her carriage in the late afternoon sun, Maria Fairgood vigorously plied her fan. She was miffed. Emily Trent had, not once, but twice today, refused to listen to perfectly good advice. And Candace had the audacity to go off with Edward Croyden, and then compounded her lapse by returning more than twenty minutes late to the White Lion. She *had* apologized, but Maria suspected the girl was not at all sincere. Had she been the least repentant, Candace would not have been laughing and conversing almost exclusively with Mr. Croyden during the luncheon.

And now, while Maria sat waiting impatiently, they insisted on traipsing all about the ruins of the ancient church tower. Only Jasper had shown any regard for her comfort. She was of a mind to have him drive her home at once. Candace, if she did not choose to come with them, could return with the vicarage party. The more Maria thought of it, the more appealing the idea became. She peered up at the top of the hill, hoping to espy her son.

When she saw him approaching a few moments later, she leaned her head back against the squibs and closed her eyes.

"Mother? Are you feeling ill, Mother?" Jasper asked with considerable concern.

"A megrim," she murmured, allowing her eyes to flutter open and slowly lifting her head. "I fear I am getting too old to withstand the heat, but do not give me a thought. You go along with your friends, Jasper."

"I cannot leave you here like this, Mother," he said, but his voice sounded indecisive and his gaze strayed to the church tower, where the sounds of high-pitched laughter echoed among the ruins.

Annoyed, Maria leaned her head back again and gave a small moan. When she had her son's full attention, she said in a weak, barely audible voice, "I hate to be a trouble to you, but perhaps it would be best if you drove me home now."

"Of course, Mother. I am sorry you do not feel well. Just rest for a moment while I fetch Candace."

"Oh, Jasper, do not spoil her day, too. Leave her stay. She can return with her aunt."

"Perhaps that would be best," he reluctantly agreed, and hurried off to find the others. By the time he'd climbed the hill again, he was sweating profusely, and could sympathize with his mother. It was really too hot for such an excursion. He found the party from the vicarage on the far side of the ruins, observing the view of the valley spread out below them. Amazing, he thought, how Candace managed to look so cool. Even Croyden did not appear to mind the heat, though with his dark complexion, one could surmise he spent a great deal of time outdoors. No doubt, he was accustomed to such weather.

"Jasper, do come look," Candace invited as she caught sight of him. "The view is worth the climb."

He gave the sweep of green, rolling fields and leafy trees in the valley below a cursory glance. Nothing exceptional, in his opinion, but he nodded. "Very pretty. Candace, I regret to tell you that Mother is not feeling at all well."

"Oh, dear," Emily said. "I thought her color looked a bit off at the inn. Shall I go to her?"

He shook his head. "Thank you, but I doubt there is anything you could do. She wants only to go home."

"I shall come at once," Candace said.

"Your willingness does you credit, my dear, but you know how thoughtful Mother is, and she does not wish to spoil your day. Would it be possible for you to drive home with the others? I know you will be somewhat crowded, but—"

"Nothing simpler," Croyden interrupted. "I shall ride on the box with the driver, and Miss Stafford may have my seat. Please convey my sympathy to your mother."

Feeling much as if he'd been dismissed, Jasper said, "Well, then, I suppose I had best be off. I will call tomorrow, if you will be at home, and let you know how mother does." He thanked Croyden for the luncheon, took his leave of Mrs. Trent, and with nothing left to detain him, turned and started the trudge back down the hill. Twice he looked back, but the small group had passed beyond the stone walls, and he could see nothing of them.

"A lovely day," Emily declared quietly as their carriage turned on High Street late that afternoon, but it had been a long one and Theresa's head rested sleepily against her shoulder. "I cannot remember when I have enjoyed an outing so much. We must all express our gratitude to Mr. Croyden."

"He is so droll," Thomasina declared. "A pity he is so old."

Candace stared at her, surprised. "Old? Why, he cannot be above five-and-twenty."

"Do you think? He seems much older, and sometimes he treats me as though I were a mere child."

Emily frowned at her. "Perhaps that is because you sometimes behave like one. I am not at all pleased with your conduct today, Thomasina, and if you do not cease flirting with Mr. Croyden at every opportunity, I shall have to speak to your father."

"Oh, Mama, I am only practicing for when we go to London. Mr. Croyden knows that."

"That may be, but Mrs. Fairgood does not, and she told me this afternoon she thought your behavior most unbecoming, and if she did not know you, she would not hesitate to deem you *fast*."

"Surely you are not going to listen to her," Thomasina said with a pout. "She finds fault with everyone—even Candace."

Her cousin raised her brows. "Does she, indeed?"

Thomasina laughed. "Were your ears not burning this afternoon? One would have thought you had eloped with Mr. Croyden the way she—"

"That is enough," Emily ordered, glaring at her eldest daughter. Turning to Candace, she said, "Maria was annoyed at being kept waiting, and she seems to have taken Mr. Croyden in dislike. Under the circumstances, I do not think her remarks bear repeating."

Candace might have questioned her further, but the carriage swept into the vicarage drive. Emily woke her youngest daughter, and a moment later

134

Croyden appeared at the door to assist the ladies to alight.

As he helped Emily down, then Theresa, Thomasina nudged her cousin and whispered, "If you want to keep Jasper as a beau, you'd better make amends with the old lady."

"Jasper must make his own decisions."

"Ha! He will do what she tells him, and if it was me, I would as lief marry the stable lad than have her for a mother-in-law." She turned as Croyden reappeared and gave him her hand. Mindful of her mother's watchful eye, she murmured politely, "Thank you, sir, for an utterly delightful day."

"The pleasure was mine," he said gravely, but his eyes sparkled with amusement.

He helped Candace down, then reached into the boot for the bundles he had stored there. In addition to his own purchases, there were packages of ribbons, new gloves for Theresa, a length of fine silk, and a straw bonnet that Thomasina had persuaded her mother to buy her.

Jonathan came out to greet his family and laughed as he saw Croyden's laden arms. "Well, it appears the ladies had a successful day shopping. You must be quite exhausted. I hope you will stay and dine with us."

"Thank you, sir. I would be honored."

Emily, helping to sort their purchases, smiled at her husband. "You need not think we bankrupted you, sir. Most of these belong to Mr. Croyden. He has been quite mysterious about what he bought."

"A few trinkets," he told the reverend, "but I should like your advice. Might I have a word with you?"

"Why, certainly," Jonathan replied, somewhat

surprised. "Come into the library. I daresay a bit of brandy would not go amiss?"

"It would be most welcome," Damian replied truthfully, and while the ladies went abovestairs to change their dresses, the gentlemen settled comfortably in tall wing chairs, brandy and glasses on the inlaid table between them.

As much as he cherished the ladies in his family, Jonathan occasionally yearned for another man with whom he could enjoy a rational conversation. There were no such men in Thatchwood. The squire, when he'd been at home, tended to fall asleep if the talk ventured beyond horses and hunting. Sir Bakersfield, supposedly an educated gentleman, unfortunately lacked sufficient common sense to find his own way home. As for Jasper Fairgood, his opinionated and narrow-minded discourse allowed little room for discussion. Mr. Croyden, however, was a man of wide-ranging interests and considerable learning, and Jonathan quite looked forward to the evening ahead.

It was pleasant in the library with the doors standing open to capture the cool breeze. It drifted in, fluttering the curtains, and carrying the fresh scent of roses which mingled nicely with the beeswax Mary had applied that morning to the old book cabinets. Beyond the room, the muted sounds of the ladies could be heard, their voices lifting and dipping as they discussed the day. Jonathan sipped his brandy and felt content.

One glass led to another, and by the time the gentlemen were called to dinner, the decanter stood empty. Jonathan had only the haziest recollection of their conversation, but he did recall agreeing that, of course, Edward Croyden must consider himself part of the family.

Thus it was that when the ladies came down to breakfast the following morning, each found a distinctively wrapped package from Crandle & Bailey's beside her plate.

Jonathan, at the head of the table, enjoyed their surprise, and when they were all seated, explained, "Mr. Croyden is deeply appreciative of the hospitality we have extended him, and wished to express his gratitude with a small token. He very properly sought my permission, as the gifts he chose are outside the bounds of what would normally be considered proper for a gentleman to give a lady."

Thomasina looked intrigued, and Theresa, her fingers itching to undo the wrapping of the tiny box beside her plate, asked, "May we open them now, Papa?"

"You may, unless you wish to wait until after breakfast," he replied teasingly, but the words were hardly out of his mouth before his daughters tore open the wrappings.

Amid the pleased cries of surprise and rapture, Candace slowly unwrapped the tiny shepherdess. A wave of pure delight washed over her. He did buy me flowers, she thought as her fingers caressed the exquisitely wrought nosegay of roses the dainty shepherdess held in her hand. Candace had admired the figure in the shop as she would have any work of art, or the sunset, or the evening stars . . . thinking it beautiful, but knowing it to be far beyond her reach. She wondered if her uncle had any notion of how steep was the price, and glanced up at him.

Jonathan, however, was engrossed in examining

his own gift. He knew what the others were receiving, but his own was a surprise and one that pleased him greatly. He touched the weathered face of Paul, amazed that an artist could so perfectly capture the passion of the disciple as he preached. "Emily, my dear, do look at this. If I am not mistaken, it is very like the one Bishop Harleigh has on his desk."

She agreed it was lovely, and showed him her gold cross. "Dare I accept it? It is one of the finest I have ever seen."

"I pondered the matter for some time last evening. Mr. Croyden is most persuasive," he said, omitting to mention the amount of brandy they'd consumed in the process.

"Then we may keep them, Papa?" Thomasina asked, holding the tourmaline up to admire the way the sun reflected off it. She could hardly wait to see the effect against her cloak.

"Please, Papa?" Theresa coaxed. She had never owned anything so exquisite.

Jonathan reluctantly nodded. The presents Croyden had chosen appeared much more expensive and impressive this morning than the "mere trinkets and baubles" that gentleman had shown him in the library the night before. But it was too late now to go back on his word.

Candace, under the pretext of visiting Mrs. Bellweather, rode out as soon as possible after breakfast to deliver Harry's money. Despite the sunny weather, her spirits were subdued. She adored the figure of the tiny shepherdess that now reposed on the dressing table in her room, but every time she saw it, she thought of Edward Croyden.

He had somehow inveigled his way past her guard and crept into her heart. She knew it was foolish of her. He was a rogue, a scoundrel, and a liar. How could she care for someone who made a mockery of all she believed in? It should not matter that he was also charming and amusing, and had a way of listening to her as though what she said was important to him. Apparently she was more like her mother than she had imagined, ready to cast aside the devotion of a good man for the fleeting attention of a rake, a master of deception. She wished she had never met him.

Until Edward Croyden rode into her life, she'd been reasonably content. Jasper Fairgood might pale in comparison, but he was kind, thoughtful, and considerate. It had not seemed terribly important that he was somewhat somber of nature and rather opinionated. And while the prospect of marrying him had not precisely gladdened her heart, neither had it repulsed her, as it did now.

Last night she had considered Thomasina's advice to make amends with Mrs. Fairgood. Her cousin, at times, had a perceptiveness that surprised Candace. She knew the advice was good, and she also knew she would not take it. Even the knowledge that Edward Croyden would ride out of her life as easily as he had appeared, and she would likely never see him again, did not have the power to change the way she felt. She remembered Mrs. Bellweather saying that once one had tasted a fine champagne, one would never again be content with mere sherry. Croyden was champagne.

The thought was sobering. Dismounting, she tied Garnet to a shrub and, carrying the small wrapped bundle of bread and cheese she'd brought for Harry, walked the rest of the way to the gamekeeper's hut while trying very hard not to think of Croyden. As she stepped into the small clearing, she softly called Harry's name. When she didn't receive an answering hail, she glanced about uneasily.

The woods were quiet, peaceful, as only a forest can be in the early morning. In the distance she could hear the squawk of birds and chatter of squirrels, but in the glade nothing stirred. Candace eyed the hut. It had an abandoned air, the door loose on its hinges and standing slightly ajar, just as it had when she'd first brought Harry there.

Cautiously, she crept closer and listened for a moment before pushing the door wide. Empty. She stepped inside and glanced around, her nose wrinkling at the pungent aroma that lingered in the room. Except for the rancid odor, nothing seemed out of place.

Now what, she wondered. She had warned Harry to stay close to the hut. It was too dangerous for him to go wandering about on his own.

"Eureka! Got him!"

The jubilant cry came from near the stream. Recognizing Harry's voice, Candace followed the narrow, winding path down to the water. She spotted him, standing knee-deep in the stream, his back to her.

"Harry!"

He glanced around, but only for a second. "Come on down," he called over his shoulder. "Wait till you see this."

This proved to be a twelve-inch trout, all shiny and speckled, which Harry was in the process of releasing from his hook. "It took me all morning, but I caught him," he told her proudly. "Caught one yesterday, too, which I had for dinner. I never knew fish could taste so good."

"Yes, well, that's nice, but I came to tell—"

"Nice?" he yelled, outraged. "Is that all you can say? *That's nice, Harry,* when I struggled for better than two hours, and with a bad arm at that. Let me tell you something, Candace Stafford, *nice* does not begin to do justice to this fellow."

He held up the fish, which was, she admitted, a fine specimen. But his expression was so comical, she couldn't help smiling. "He's wonderful, Harry, and you are to be commended for catching him— but do come out. I came to tell you that I have the money for you."

"Oh—that's grand," he said, but without any notable enthusiasm. He looked sorrowfully at the fish in his hand. "I guess I should throw him back. Seems a shame after all the trouble I went through to catch him."

She watched him reluctantly toss the trout in the water with a splash that sent a spray shooting upward, and spread a ripple effect across the surface. Harry stared after the fish for a moment, then trudged up the bank. "I'll tell you what, Candace. I never knew fishing could be such a good sport. When I get my affairs untangled, I think I shall come back here and try it again."

"And stay in the gamekeeper's cottage?"

"Well, maybe the inn, though the old place is beginning to seem like home."

"You have been out here too long," she teased as they walked back up the path together.

When they were back inside the hut, she untied her reticule and withdrew a bundle of notes. "I sold your ring at Crandle & Bailey's in Heptonstall. Mr.

141

Crandle was very generous. He said the stone was exceptionally fine."

Harry, his blue eyes clouding for a moment, nodded. "Gad, I hated to part with it, but I mean to buy it back. And I mean to repay you, too, for all you have done. Did you have much trouble getting away?"

"Not much," she murmured, busying herself with unwrapping the bread and cheese. She passed it to him and added quietly, "Mr. Croyden very obligingly volunteered to take my aunt and my cousins shopping in Heptonstall, and to visit the old ruins there. He was . . . most helpful."

Alarmed, Harry demanded, "He didn't see the ring, did he?"

"No, I was careful, but—Harry, he does not seem like a villain to me. Are you certain he means you harm?"

Nearly choking on a hunk of bread, Harry coughed and sputtered till he got his breath back. "Gad, where did you get such a notion? I never said he meant me harm."

She stared at him, unable to believe what she was hearing. Making an effort to control her temper, she stated with quiet fury, "You *said* that I must not let him see your ring. You *said* that I must not let him know your whereabouts."

"But only because he knows me," Harry protested, backing up as she advanced toward him.

"You *said* you did not trust him."

"Now, Candace, I never said that. I may have said I did not trust anyone at present, but—"

"Oh, you—you idiot! You deserve that someone shot you," she fumed. Fearing that she might lose

142

her temper completely and throw something at him, she strode outside.

Harry followed her. "I don't understand why you are so angry."

She whirled around to face him. "Because I have been imagining Mr. Croyden as some dangerous villain, and he has been so kind, and he . . ." Her words trailed off as a new thought struck her. "Harry, if he does not intend you harm, then why is he searching for you, and why will you not let him help you?"

"I don't need his help," he insisted stubbornly. "And I don't know why Croyden's looking for me. I would think he had better things to do with his time."

"Then you don't believe he is any danger to you?"

"No—but he's officious and interfering and always thinks he knows best. I don't want him interfering in my affairs."

"But why should he?"

"For heaven's sake, you are like a dog worrying over a bone. Forget Croyden. I am leaving today, and once I am gone, he'll likely disappear, too."

"For which I will be doubly thankful," she retorted. "Good-bye, Mr. Reynald. It has been delightful."

"Candace, wait," he called after her as she turned and headed for the path, but she ignored him. Running, he caught up with her. "Candace, please do not leave like this."

She continued striding down the path, and he awkwardly followed along behind her, for it was wide enough only for one. "Listen, I am sorry if I offended you. I know how much I stand in your debt, and when I come back—"

"Do not," she muttered furiously as they approached the point where the path bisected with the wider trail, and she had tethered Garnet.

"Do not what?"

She untied the reins and turned to face him. "If you wish to repay me, then do not come back here. You have turned my life upside down. Because of you I have deceived my aunt and uncle, told more lies than I ever have in my life, and then you have the unmitigated gall to compare me to a dog—oh, drat." She reached up a hand to brush away the sudden tears brimming in her eyes.

"Aw, Candace, don't cry," he pleaded. He placed his good arm around her and drew her to him, and soothingly patted her back. "I didn't mean to say you were like a dog."

"You did." She sniffed against his shoulder.

"Well, maybe a little, but I have got a mastiff at home, and he is my best friend. I think very highly of dogs."

A gurgle, part sob, part laughter, escaped her. She stepped back and looked up at him. "You are an odious boy, and I do not know why I tried to help you."

"I don't, either, but I am glad you did. I hate to think of the fix I would be in if it were not for you. Will you forgive me? Are we still friends?"

"Friends," she agreed.

"And you won't mind if I come back? I should really like to try fishing again when I've got the use of both arms."

"Harry! Is that all you can think of?"

"No, my stomach has been rumbling for an hour. I am starving. Will you come back to the hut?"

She shook her head. "I cannot. I must get back to

144

the vicarage, and you should rest after you eat. You will have a care, won't you? After all my trouble, I should hate for anything to happen to you."

He nodded, then leaned down to kiss her cheek. "Thank you for everything, Candace. I shall see you in a fortnight."

She nodded, afraid that if she tried to speak, she would start crying again. She started to step away, but she heard a rustling in the woods behind them. Looking around, she gazed into Jasper Fairgood's angry eyes.

He looked from Harry to Candace, then demanded, "May I ask what the devil you mean by meeting this fellow in the woods?"

"And who the devil might you be?" Harry growled, stepping in front of Candace in an effort to shield her.

"I, sir, am engaged to the young lady you were mauling. I believe that gives me the right to ask certain questions."

Were it not all so horrible, Candace would have collapsed in a fit of giggles at the sight of Harry struggling to defend her with one good arm, and Jasper playing the outraged suitor.

Chapter 10

"Then where is his horse?" Jasper demanded as he and Candace rode out of the woods.

"I have not the least notion," she replied, close to losing patience. "I told you—when I met the gentleman, he was wandering around, obviously lost. He said he was not feeling well and had taken a tumble, apparently hitting his head. When he regained consciousness, his horse was gone and he no idea where he was. I merely stopped to make certain he was not hurt, and gave him directions."

"Directions to where?"

"To the stream," she said, thinking fast. "He thought perhaps his horse might have wandered away in search of water."

"I see, and he was naturally so overcome with gratitude that he felt compelled to kiss you."

"You are mistaken, Jasper. He did not kiss me. It may have looked that way, but he merely lost his balance and stumbled against me."

She sounded so positive, he almost believed her. He *wanted* to believe her, but he could not dismiss the evidence of his eyes. He had very clearly seen the young man lean down and kiss her cheek. The fellow had not stumbled at all, and the ease of the gesture bespoke of familiarity. He wondered how long she had been secretly meeting him. And how far their intimacy had progressed.

The thought pained him. For several years he had taken it for granted that one day Candace would become Mrs. Jasper Fairgood. Because of her modesty, her devotion to the church, and her genteel manners, he had deemed her worthy of the honor. But now—to find her dallying in the woods with a young man, and to hear her brazenly lying about it—this was not the conduct of a well-bred lady. He had been grossly deceived.

He glanced at Candace, trying to discern in what manner she had changed, for she was obviously not the same girl he had courted for the past two years. Or had she deceived him all along? He recalled the numerous times his mother had occasion to criticize Candace, small things to be sure, which he had not thought important at the time. But perhaps his own infatuation had blinded him to her true nature.

"Why are you staring at me," she demanded, a rush of color flooding her cheeks.

"I thought I knew you," he said sadly, "but it appears I was grievously mistaken. Your conduct with Croyden yesterday was sufficiently unbecoming to give me pause as to the wisdom of making you my wife. However, I was fully prepared, in view of our long relationship, and the understanding between us, to give you the benefit of doubt. But now you try to foist this ... this Banbury tale off on me when it is quite apparent you've been secretly meeting that man—well, I can only conclude that Mother was right. Breeding will tell."

Fury blazing in her eyes, Candace drew Garnet

to a halt. "What precisely do you mean by that remark?"

Jasper flushed, but with an air of righteousness he replied, "If you insist on plain speaking, then I can only say that it seems clear you are determined to follow in your mother's footsteps, which, I must add, disappoints me greatly. When I think of the trust I reposed in you, of my willingness to overlook the scandal attached to your name—"

"You need not overlook anything, Jasper," she interrupted with deadly calm. "You are mistaken about a number of things, not the least of which is the notion that we are, or ever have been, betrothed. We are not, and since we are not, my conduct is none of your concern. Go home to your mother. I have no doubt that she will applaud your decision."

Her unexpected anger shocked him. He had expected tears and apologies, and had been prepared to be magnanimous once she realized the magnitude of her mistake and was properly remorseful, but she was not in the least repentant. Indeed, the way she lashed out at him, one would think *he* was at fault.

Jasper hauled on the reins as his horse tried to brush him against a tree. The morning was not going at all the way he had imagined. He twisted around in the saddle to face Candace, and warned her, "You are making a terrible mistake, which I do not think you fully realize. However, if you behave sensibly, I am sure—"

"The problem is, I have behaved *sensibly* for too long," she said, cutting off his protests. "It is clear we will not suit, and there is no more to be said."

"Well! If that is the way you feel—"

"I do. Good-bye, Jasper." She turned Garnet and headed back toward the woods, unable to bear the sight of him a moment longer, and wanting only to be alone.

"Where are you going?" he called. "Back to him? Ha! You will soon find out he won't marry you, either."

Keeping her back straight and chin lifted high, she ignored him. Anger suffused her cheeks with color, but it was tempered by the knowledge that she, too, was at fault. She should have spoken to Jasper sooner—made him understand that they were not *unofficially engaged*, as he so often told everyone. She should have made it clear to him that she had never agreed to wed him, and never would.

She had tried, she told herself, but every time she'd attempted to make her feelings known, Jasper had brushed her objections aside. Now, instead of parting on amicable terms as she had intended, he was angry—perhaps angry enough to spread the story of her meeting Harry throughout the village.

She could imagine the looks she would receive, and the gossip that would spread like wildfire through the village. Uncle Jonathan and Aunt Emily would be so disappointed in her, and Mrs. Fairgood would be unbearable.

Dispirited, she turned Garnet on the bridle path. She had chosen the long way around only to avoid further conversation with Jasper, for despite his suspicions, she had no desire to see Harry again—or, indeed, anyone. Had she not promised Mrs. Bellweather she would stop by, Candace would have ridden home and sought the sanctuary of her room.

She allowed Garnet to meander at her own pace,

hoping the ride through the peaceful woods would help to restore her usual serenity. However, when she arrived at Mrs. Bellweather's, she still felt as though the world conspired against her. Not even the heady scent of roses had the power to lift her spirits.

Young Darby, weeding the narrow bed that curved along the drive, dropped his spade and came running to take her horse.

"Do not bother putting her in the shed," Candace told him. "I shall be only a few moments."

"Yes, miss. Can I ride 'er a bit?"

"If you do not neglect your work for long," Candace said, giving the towheaded boy a wan smile. She knew he loved horses as much as his mistress loved her flowers. Even an old mare like Garnet enchanted him.

Annie was waiting for her at the door. "Mrs. B. has been on the watch for you, miss. She's in the sitting room and said you was to go right in."

"Thank you, Annie," Candace said as she followed the girl down the long hall, careful to step over the tomcat sprawled in the doorway. Mrs. Bellweather was in her usual chair in front of the window, chuckling as she watched Darby ride off.

"That boy's a terrible gardener, but he's a natural-born horseman. Pity he can't have a mount of his own. Well, perhaps if he stays with me long enough, I shall buy him one."

"You must not consider such a thing," Candace warned, knowing the older woman could ill afford such a generous gesture.

Maude glanced up at her. "Child, if I've learned one thing in all my years, it's that doing for others is the only true way to find happiness."

"But the expense—"

"Fiddle. There's some things that you can't put a price on, and happiness is one of 'em. And speaking of which, you look as sad as a cat caught in the rain. Sit down, child, sit down, and unbutton your lip. What is troubling you?"

Candace sank into the tall chair opposite. "I am supposed to cheer you, Mrs. Bellweather, not the other way around."

"Then tell me what has caused that long face, and I shall give you the benefit of my advice. I adore giving advice—cheers me up no end." She poured a cup of tea as she spoke, and handed it to Candace. "Drink that, my dear, and you will feel better, though if you were not the vicar's niece, I would give you champagne instead."

Champagne, Candace thought. *Edward Croyden was champagne, and not suitable for the vicar's niece, either.* Sudden tears dampened her eyes, and a tightness in the back of her throat made it impossible to speak.

"Why, my dear, you are crying. What is it, child?" Maude asked softly as she reached out a gnarled hand and gently patted her guest on the shoulder. "Can you tell me?"

The warm sympathy in the older woman's voice was Candace's undoing. The tears that had threatened all morning overflowed. She blindly accepted the handkerchief Mrs. Bellweather offered, and wiped at her eyes.

"Take your time, darling. Cry it out, and you will feel better."

"I am sorry," Candace murmured when she had regained a small measure of control. Feeling she owed her hostess an explanation of some sort, she added, "It has been a . . . a difficult morning. Jasper and I had a disagreement."

"Surely, you are not crying over him? Why, he is not worth the tip of your little finger. What happened, dear? Did he say something hurtful?"

Candace nodded, and before she realized it, she was telling Mrs. Bellweather the entire story. "And the irony of it is," she finished, "had he come only a few moments later, Harry would have been gone."

"Jasper Fairgood is a pompous blatherskite, and you need not waste your tears on him. Quite frankly, my dear, you are better off without him."

That brought a watery smile to Candace's lips. "I do not care that Jasper no longer wishes to marry me, but I am worried about what he may say. It is so unfair, Mrs. Bellweather. All these years I have been so careful not to give anyone the slightest cause to say I was like my mother . . . and now, simply because I befriended a young man in need of help—"

"I would have likely done the same had I stood in your shoes, Candace, though doubtless I would have enjoyed it more. Was he handsome, your Harry?"

She laughed. "I suppose one might think so, but mostly he reminded me of my brother."

"And Edward Croyden?"

Candace could not help the blush that tinged her cheeks, but she did not want to discuss Croyden, not even with someone as kind and sympathetic as Mrs. Bellweather. She looked down at the cup cradled in her hands and replied carefully, "I suppose that once he learns Harry is gone, he, too, will disappear."

"Pity. I rather like him. He reminds me of my

Herbert. Well, now, we shall have to wait and see what happens. It seems to me that much depends on Jasper. For what it is worth, my dear, I do not think he will be eager to spread the tale."

"I wish I might believe so. But he was so angry."

Mrs. Bellweather nodded her white head, her tiny eyes alight with amusement. "You have not considered how badly this affair reflects on Jasper. For two years he has told anyone who would listen that the pair of you were betrothed. If he dares speak out, it will seem like mere malicious gossip because you threw him over. After all, Harry is gone, and from what you've told me, no one in the village ever saw him. Save for his mother, who would believe Jasper?"

"I pray you are right. I would hate anyone to think I am like my mother."

"But you are, my dear. You have all her best qualities and her beauty, and it is high time you stopped worrying over it. Take your hair out of that fusty bun and cease wearing those dreadfully ill-fitting gowns. You are a very pretty girl, Candace, and you have no reason to hide your beauty. Your mother made a mistake, and she paid for it with her life. Do not, I beg you, pay with yours as well."

By Monday, Candace was beginning to think Mrs. Bellweather correct in her prophecy. Apparently, Jasper had not said a word. No one looked at her accusingly, or whispered behind gloved hands when the family attended church on Sunday. And except for a noticeable coolness between her and Jasper when they met at the door afterward, no one would guess they had argued. Even Mrs. Fairgood had greeted her pleasantly, no doubt will-

ing to overlook Candace's faults now that her son
would not be marrying her.

Sunday dinner had passed quietly, and if Mr.
Croyden's lively presence was missed, no one commented on his absence. The placid, unvarying rou-
tine of the vicarage continued undisturbed through
Monday, and by evening Candace could almost
imagine that Edward Croyden and Harry Reynald
had never ventured into Thatchwood.

On Tuesday, pouring rain and sunless skies covered the vicarage. Candace, who yearned to stay in
bed and pull the covers over her head, performed
her duties competently but with such a lack of
cheerfulness that even her uncle noticed and inquired if she was not feeling well.

Candace blamed her melancholy on the weather,
but she was not the only one with low spirits. Her
aunt fretted that she had not heard from Mr.
Croyden in several days, and hoped he had not
taken ill, or been suddenly called home. However,
late in the afternoon his groom delivered a billet
assuring the Trents that he had not forgotten his
promise to escort them to the assembly. He would
call for the ladies late the following afternoon.

Candace heard the news with mixed feelings.
She had convinced herself that Edward Croyden
had somehow managed to follow Harry north, and
she would never hear from him again. She had re-
peatedly told herself it was for the best, but at
night, when her room was lit by candlelight and
she couldn't sleep, her gaze would linger on the
tiny shepherdess. The delicate figure reminded her
so poignantly of Croyden. As rain pounded the roof,
she admitted she missed him. She missed the way

he teased her, missed the verbal dueling, even the way he provoked her into losing her temper.

She fought the growing attraction she felt for him, for nothing good could come of it. He might not be the villain she had once believed him, but he had lied about why he was in Thatchwood. And if he would lie to her about that, then he would lie about other things. But even as her mind told her he could not be trusted, her heart yearned to see him again. She tried to sleep, but her thoughts were as turbulent as the rain splattering against the windows.

Uncle Jonathan had said that if the storm did not pass, he thought it would be advisable to postpone attending the assembly. The roads could be treacherous if flooding occurred, and the drive to Heptonstall was a long one. Her cousins had, for once, prayed diligently. Candace left it to fate to decide the weather.

Wednesday dawned clear and sunny, the air smelling of that peculiar sweetness that arises after a cleansing rain. The vicarage hummed with unaccustomed activity as the ladies within prepared for their evening, and even Candace was affected with an anticipation she had not thought to feel.

She spent the morning in the sewing room, altering one of her old gowns so that it more closely fit her slender figure. Her aunt sought her there, entering the room with a frown marring her usually serene brow.

"I do not understand this, Candace. Jasper Fairgood has sent his regrets that he will not be able to join us this evening, and not a word of explanation."

Candace sighed and set aside her sewing. "I am not surprised, Aunt Emily. We had a disagreement on Saturday."

"That may be, but it does not excuse his incivility in regretting an invitation he has already accepted, and on such short notice. It shall make it extremely awkward with the carriages."

"I am sorry. I should have spoken to you sooner. We have decided that we . . . we do not suit, and I am certain Jasper feels it would be awkward to provide me escort."

Emily stared at her for a moment. She had paid no attention when her niece mentioned a disagreement. The pair had disagreed on nearly everything under the sun during the past two years. But this was serious. She sat down beside Candace and took her hand. "My dear, I had no idea. Was it because I allowed you to go off with Mr. Croyden on Friday? I know Maria thought it improper of me to allow it, and if that is the reason, I could speak to her on your behalf."

"Thank you, Aunt Emily, but you are not to blame. I have known for some time that I could not marry Jasper. If anyone is at fault, I am for allowing him to believe otherwise."

Emily patted her hand. "Perhaps it is wrong of me to say so, but I confess I am vastly relieved. He may be an admirable young man, but I cannot think you would have been happy with him." She paused, looking toward the hall to be certain they were quite alone, then whispered, "Just between us, my dear, the notion of having Maria Fairgood in the family was sufficient to give me the blue devils."

Candace laughed. "Does Uncle Jonathan share your sentiments?"

Emily nodded. "But do not tell him I told you so. It troubles your uncle greatly that he cannot admire so worthy a young man. One cannot really find fault with Jasper, 'tis only that he is so . . . so earnest. But let us not speak of him. Come September, we shall all go to London, and I am certain you will have dozens of offers to choose from."

"Is it settled, then?" Candace asked, surprised. "Uncle Jonathan has agreed?"

"Not yet," Emily confided with a half-smile. "But he shall. Now I must decide what to do about carriages. Cyril Bakersfield is coming . . . perhaps I could permit Theresa to drive with him if Thomasina goes with her. Yes, I believe that might be best. Then you and I may go in Mr. Croyden's carriage." Emily left the room, murmuring to herself.

Candace smiled and resumed her sewing. But the thought of the long ride to Heptonstall, sitting opposite Edward Croyden, soon occupied her thoughts to the exclusion of all else. She thought briefly of exchanging seats with Thomasina. Her cousin would adore having Mr. Croyden's company for an hour and a half, even under the watchful eye of her mother. Trading places seemed the ideal solution, but Candace did not leave her chair. She told herself she did not want to upset Aunt Emily's arrangements.

Looking down at her sewing, she discovered her stitches had gone awry. She ripped out the seam and started anew, determined not to think anymore of smoky, dark eyes, broad shoulders, or lips that made one wonder what it would be like to be kissed. . . .

Damian sat at his ease in the taproom of the Boar's Head Inn, the remains of a substantial repast before him. He had arrived at the inn close to the noon hour, and not expected much in the way of luncheon. But Mrs. Marley, in an ecstasy of delight at seeing him return, assured him she would have a tolerable meal before him in no time. At half past twelve he sat down to a savory bouillon, rissoles of sweetbread, filet of fish, and cutlets, followed by fresh fruit and coffee.

Paddy, who had returned the evening before and spent an agonizing night wondering where his master had disappeared to, sat opposite him. Skinny elbows propped on the table, hands cupped around a mug of ale, he waited patiently for Damian to finish his meal. After Mrs. Marley had finally cleared the table and poured Damian's coffee, Paddy said, "Now can I tell you, gov?"

"I see no way to avoid it," Damian replied with a grin. "Unburden yourself."

"You wouldn't be thinking it so funny if it hadda been you the countess was shooting questions at."

"Of course not. That was entirely the point in sending you as my emissary."

"I don't know about no emissary, but she weren't a bit pleased, I can tell you, no, nor satisfied, either. It puzzles her to know why you're still in this place which she ain't never heard of, and why Master Harry came here at all."

"I had hoped my letter would serve as sufficient explanation," Damian said as he sipped his coffee.

"All I know is she had more questions than that old dog outside has fleas. And she ain't the only one," Paddy declared, warming to his list of grievances. "That bloody valet of yours tried to insist I bring him back here with me. Seems to think you can't survive without him around to dress you and such."

"Phipps does have a point." Damian sighed. He stretched out his legs and looked sadly at his Hessians. The boots would never be the same. It was doubtful that even Phipps would be able to restore their once-gleaming luster. "You will doubtless think it weak of me, but I find I rather miss having my valet. Did he pack the items I requested?"

Paddy nodded. "He did, grumbling all the while and wanting to know who was tending your shirts and coat—I thought he'd keel over when I told him how Mrs. Marley was doing for you. I tell you, gov, I had all I could do to keep him from coming back with me. Him and Siddons both, the pair of 'em blathering at me like a couple of babes in need of suckling."

"Surely not Siddons," Damian said, raising his brows. His very correct secretary rarely showed any trace of emotion.

"I suspicion he's worried, you disappearing the way you did, and he said as how there's urgent business needing your attention."

"There is always urgent business, according to Siddons. It's one of the things I most dislike about him, but worried? I cannot imagine it," Damian replied, and waved to Marley.

While the landlord refilled their drinks and wiped the table, Paddy observed his master. The gov would likely be embarrassed to know just how devoted his servants were. Most had been at Deerpark for more years than Paddy cared to remember, and each man thought he was the earl's favorite. There wasn't one of them what wouldn't lay down his life for Damian. Siddons and Phipps were in a pucker over being left behind, and Paddy knew had it been he, he'd feel the same.

When Marley had left, Damian looked across the table. "Now, what's put that long look on your face?"

"You ain't gonna like it," Paddy warned.

"Out with it, then."

"I don't think Siddons wouldda told me if Phipps hadn't let the cat out of the bag. It's like this, gov. That duke came back—the one what claimed Master Harry owes him."

"Cardiff, yes. He has much to answer for. What did His Grace want this time?"

"News of Harry, belike. He saw my lady, and Phipps said he ain't never seen her so angry. She told Creswall not to admit the duke if he comes back. Said she ain't at home to him."

"Good for Mother, but I wonder what brought the gentleman back so soon. I told him I would pay the note in thirty days if I had not heard from Harry, and we still have a week. He must be growing concerned. . . ." Damian mused.

"There's worse," Paddy said, a flush of color creeping up his leathery face. "I suspicion I was followed back here. I seen a fellow lolling about outside the stable this morning, and I'm nearly certain he's the same one I seen at Deerpark by the gate. His cart had lost a wheel, and I didn't think much of it at the time."

"Naturally not, but I find it rather interesting," Damian drawled, and though his manner appeared relaxed, his dark eyes turned as black as night. "Is the fellow still here?"

Paddy shook his head. "Leastways, not that I know. I ain't seen him since."

"Keep a sharp eye out, and let me know at once if you spot him again," Damian ordered, then stood and stretched.

"What now, gov?"

"If Mr. Marley will be so obliging, I intend to have a hot bath, shave, and change my clothes. I shall need you to drive the carriage this afternoon. We call for the ladies at the vicarage at four, so don't wander too far."

"But what about Master Harry?"

"You need not worry about him. My brother left Saturday morning and should be safely at Greenbriar by now."

"Then what are we staying here for?"

"Three reasons," Damian said. "One, I expect Harry to return in a few days, and two, unless I am much mistaken, His Grace will honor us with an appearance shortly. I wish to be here to welcome him properly."

Paddy nodded, glad he wasn't in the duke's shoes. He followed Damian to the door, thinking over his words, then scratched his head. "You said three reasons, gov. What's the other?"

Damian smiled, his eyes full of devilment as ever Master Harry's were. "The third is for my own pleasure, and none of your business."

Chapter 11

The assembly rooms at Heptonstall were reached by climbing a steep flight of stairs, turning right, and following a narrow hall to the end, where double doors stood open to the ballroom. It had little to distinguish it, but huge potted plants had been placed at intervals to disguise the barren walls, and long mirrors were hung between the tall windows on the north side, which had the effect of making the room appear larger.

On the south end, a raised platform provided space for half a dozen musicians, still fine-tuning their instruments as the vicarage party entered. Chairs lined the remaining two walls, many already occupied by a number of dowagers and chaperons who kept a sharp eye on the young ladies promenading the room.

Mr. Sylvester Halbert, the master of ceremonies, greeted the vicarage party at the door. He was a short man, of slight build, who sought to improve his appearance by the judicious use of padding beneath his black cutaway coat, an extremely high and heavily starched collar that prevented him turning his neck more than an inch or two, sawdust to add bulk to the yellow pantaloons hugging his skinny legs, and high-heeled, jeweled pumps.

His shoes added a few inches to his height, but made him appear to lean forward as he trotted about the room performing his introductions.

He was tireless in executing his duties—too much so, Damian thought as he watched Candace stroll down the length of the room with a dark-haired young gentleman whom Halbert had presented to her. Damian knew she looked different tonight, but it had taken him some time to realize it was not just the becoming gown she wore, although that was attractive.

The slip of apple green satin hugged her shoulders and caressed her bodice beneath an overdress of patent net. The long sleeves were laced with green satin and a matching ribbon held her long curls back. For once she had dispensed with the tightly woven bun she normally favored, and tiny tendrils of curls softly framed her face. She had even worn the pearls her mother had left her, their luster gleaming against the delicate lines of her throat.

Damian watched her laugh as she gazed attentively up at her escort, and felt a flash of annoyance. She didn't have to look quite so provocatively at the young man, and what on earth was the matter with the fellow that he looked at her bosom as though he'd never seen one before?

"Mr. Croyden?"

Damian glanced down at the young lady by his side. Mr. Halbert had introduced him to her, but at the moment he could not recall her name. He smiled apologetically. "I beg your pardon, I fear my attention wandered for just a moment."

"Is she a friend of yours?" the petite blond asked, amusement shimmering in her pretty blue eyes.

"Who?"

"The young lady you were observing so intently. The one in the green gown walking with Christian Tyler."

"Are you acquainted with the gentleman?" he asked, unaware that he sounded as though he would like very much to strangle the fellow.

His diminutive partner laughed. "He is my brother, sir, and I assure you, a perfect gentleman. You need not worry—she will come to no harm with him."

"You are most perceptive," Damian replied as he guided Miss Tyler to their position in the line forming for the opening minuet. Realizing he sounded like the worst sort of boor, he added, "I do apologize for my distraction. 'Tis only that the young lady is my guest, and I feel somewhat responsible for her. This is her first assembly."

"Of course," Regina Tyler replied agreeably, but she made up her mind not to waste her smiles on Mr. Croyden, as his affections were obviously already engaged.

On the opposite side of the room, Candace took her place, hoping that she could remember the steps. Aunt Emily had engaged a dancing master two years before, when Mrs. Caldwalder had announced her intention of giving a small party in honor of her visiting niece, with dancing afterward.

Candace and her cousins had quickly learned the steps of the minuet, the quadrille, and the contredanse. The Scotch reels and the ecossaise were also approved, but Uncle Jonathan had drawn the line at his family performing the waltz. Since then, the girls had practiced with one another occasionally, but that was hardly the same as dancing with a gentleman.

Candace glanced at Theresa, who stood a few paces away from her, and who showed no signs of nervousness at all. Nor did Thomasina, who seemed intent on practicing her flirtatious glances with the tall young redhead opposite her. How could they be so calm, Candace wondered, knowing the palms of her own hands were damp beneath the white gloves she wore.

At Mr. Halbert's signal, the orchestra began playing. She accepted her partner's raised hand as she sank into a graceful curtsy. Then all else was forgotten as the music brought to mind the pattern of steps as easily as though she'd danced only yesterday. Her slippered feet moved in three-quarter time, her green eyes sparkled, and her lips curved slightly up at the corners in pure enjoyment.

As she gained confidence, Candace glanced around the ballroom. Her gaze encountered Edward Croyden, and she nearly missed her footing. She had promised to stand up with him for a quadrille later in the evening, although the idea of dancing with him made her uneasy, and she couldn't help wondering why he had asked her.

Harry was gone. If Mr. Croyden knew that, and his own suspicious disappearance at the same time convinced Candace that he did, then there could be little point in continuing his pretext of friendship with her family. Yet he had been all charm and affability in the carriage, entertaining her aunt with outrageous stories of the nobility.

I always keep my promises. She could almost hear his deep voice whispering those words in her ear. Was that the reason for his return to

Thatchwood? Some odd notion of keeping his word to Aunt Emily? But if that was so, then he would need not stay after that night, and she had clearly heard him tell her aunt he expected to remain at the Boar's Head Inn for another week, perhaps two.

She executed a turn, smiled at Mr. Tyler, and stole another glance at Edward Croyden. His attention was focused on the blond girl he'd led out, and Candace was able to study him for a moment or two. One would not think him a disreputable rogue to look at him, she thought, admiring the cut of his formal black cutaway coat. With it he wore the de rigueur white waistcoat, buff knee breeches, black silk stockings, and low-heeled black pumps with a small but distinctive jeweled buckle. If she did not know him, she would have thought him most elegant.

Sensing the regard of her own partner, Candace brought her attention back to Mr. Tyler, and smiled up at him.

"I understand this is the first time you have visited the assembly rooms. I hope you will have an enjoyable evening, so that it will not be the last."

"Thank you, Mr. Tyler," she replied as they turned for the closing steps of the minuet. "Unfortunately, my cousins and I live some distance, which makes attendance difficult."

He agreed the location of the assembly rooms was unfortunate, as he and his sister traveled above an hour to attend. He and Candace discovered they both resided in small villages and discussed the disadvantages of country life as he escorted her back to the chairs where her aunt waited.

Their conversation was of the most trivial nature, but Damian, observing the pair from the far side of the room, could see only her dark head tilted toward Tyler, her grave eyes focused on him as she listened intently.

Emily Trent watched happily as her daughters and niece circled the floor. She knew it was probably a sin, but she could not help thinking her girls the loveliest present. And they had stood up for every dance.

She scanned the room until she caught sight of Mr. Croyden. Satisfaction lit her eyes, and she smiled with the secret pleasure of knowing her instincts were correct. At first, she had cherished hopes that he and Thomasina might make a match of it, but it was clear they would not suit. Her eldest child did not **have** the sense of a butterfly and lacked the wit to appreciate a gentleman with the sophisticated charm of Edward Croyden.

Her niece, however, was far more sensible, and though she might not admit it, Candace showed every sign of being enamored. She had even made it clear to Jasper Fairgood that they were not betrothed, a step Emily heartily approved, and which she believed her niece would not have troubled to take were it not for the arrival of Mr. Croyden on the scene.

Emily had discussed the prospect of a match between the two with her husband, but Jonathan had warned her not to make too much of Croyden's kindness to the family. He reminded her that the gentleman had not asked for permission to call on Candace, and despite his own liking for the man, they really knew very little about him.

Emily knew enough—one could never mistake good breeding—although she had not said so to her husband. Heavens, if it were left to men to decide such matters, no marriages would ever be made. She watched Mr. Croyden as he danced with a drab of a girl. Such kindness, such consideration. Unlike some men, who attended balls or assemblies, and though they could dance did not. Instead, they lounged in halls or doorways, looking as though there was not a lady present worth dancing with. Ill-bred, she called it.

Mr. Croyden did his duty, even beyond, and sought out the shy girls and the plain ones, who might have been left without a partner. And who was to blame him if while he danced his gaze strayed after Candace.

"I believe I have the honor of this dance," Edward Croyden said, bowing before Candace as the sets for the quadrille were forming.

She smiled at him, accepting the arm he offered, though her lips and hand trembled slightly, and even her heart seemed to be doing its own version of the Highland fling beneath the bodice of her gown.

"Now, what has occurred to put that apprehensive look in your eyes?" he teased. "You seemed at ease with me in the carriage, and I cannot have said anything to offend you since our arrival, for I have not had an opportunity to speak a word with you, surrounded as you have been by admirers. Do you perhaps fear I will step on your toes?"

She gave a small gurgle of laughter. "I have seen you dancing, sir, and have no fear on that score."

"What, then?" he asked as they took their places at the far end of the diamond forming the square.

How could she answer him? Confess that he played havoc with her emotions, that when he was away, she ached to see him again, and when he was present, she wished he would disappear? Tell him that he frightened her, because he awoke yearnings that were surely improper in a young lady of breeding? Admit that she had some glimmering now of how her mother might have been tempted to leave her home and family....

"Is it this trouble with Harry?" he asked as their hands touched and formed an arch above their heads.

She glanced up as she took two tiny steps forward, and then back again. His dark eyes were filled with a whimsical humor and something akin to admiration, which sent spirals of warmth curling through her and wrapping around her heart. Her lashes swept down, hiding the confusion she felt. "I ... I do not know what you mean."

"Ah, you still do not trust me."

He said it lightly, but the underlying disappointment in his voice tore at her, shredding her conscience and the defenses she had built against his charm. She owed him nothing, but still she wanted to erase that melancholy sadness from his voice, and she offered what little comfort she could. "I do not believe you intend anyone harm, if that is what you mean."

"It is not, but it shall have to do," he said as she turned beneath his arm. He waited till she faced him again, and added, "One day, Miss Stafford, when all this nonsense is behind us, you shall admit you were wrong not to trust me."

She linked her arm in his as they slowly prome-
naded to the center of the diamond, then back
again. She kept her eyes down, but the soft voice
that floated up to him was a mixture of hope and
doubt.

"I should be pleased to make such an admission,
if it were true, Mr. Croyden."

"Blast Harry," Damian muttered beneath his
breath as Candace's slender figure circled around
him in the fifth and final figure of the quadrille. He
longed to tell her the truth, longed to hear his true
name on her lips. Every time she said *Mr. Croyden*
in that precise way of hers, he had to control an
urge to tell her everything. And yet he was not at
all certain that the Earl of Doncaster would be any
more acceptable in her eyes than plain Mr.
Croyden.

He could only pray that once she heard the reasons he traveled incognito, she would understand.
A week, a fortnight at most, and this damnable
business with Harry would be over. If Paddy's information was correct, His Grace, the Duke of Cardiff, should put in an appearance very soon. He
would arrive in Thatchwood, expecting to find
Harry . . . only Damian would be the one to confront him. He sighed, hoping all would go as he had
planned. Once he was certain his brother was safe,
then he could speak to Jonathan Trent, and trust
in the good reverend to intercede on his behalf.

"Thank you," Candace murmured later that evening as she accepted a glass of lemonade from a
tall, lanky young man. Mr. Eversleigh had partnered her in a Scottish reel, and while he danced
with enthusiasm, he unfortunately lacked a sense

of rhythm and had consequently stepped on her slippered feet several times.

When he approached her a second time, she had politely declined to dance, but softened her refusal with the suggestion that they converse instead. Mr. Eversleigh agreed promptly and guided her to a secluded alcove, where she sank gratefully onto a small settee. It was frequently overlooked by the habitués, as a large pillar blocked the view of the dance floor, and any young lady seated there would likely not be seen. It suited Candace perfectly, though she wished she could slip off her shoes for a moment and rub her aching feet.

As that was not possible, she smiled up at her escort. "Do you attend the assemblies often, Mr. Eversleigh?"

"Every week," he said, then added sheepishly, "I keep thinking that if I dance often enough, I shall get better, but my mother says I've two left feet. Pity, for I do like to dance."

Candace nodded sympathetically. "I know precisely what you mean. With me, 'tis singing. I love music, but my uncle says that all my notes sound alike, and my cousins tease me unmercifully. 'Tis vexing, for every young lady is expected to either play the pianoforte or sing, and I can do neither. Yet there are times when I am feeling particularly happy, and I cannot help singing just a little, though I do try to make certain that I am quite alone."

"Really?" he asked, much impressed. "But you should not let it worry you, Miss Stafford. Anyone who dances so beautifully should not care a fig about singing."

"You are kind to say so, but I think you would do

well to heed your own advice." When he looked puzzled, she added, "I am certain that, although you may not be as adept as you would like on the dance floor, there are other things you do admirably."

"By Jove, I never thought of it like that, but you are right. My father says I drive to an inch, and even my brother admits I am a bruising rider."

"Then you should not care a fig about dancing," she teased while smiling at his boyish enthusiasm.

"I shall try to remember that—and the next time I trample a lady's slippers, I shall apologize and tell her I am much more at home on a horse. Speaking of which, will you allow me to make amends and take you for a drive one afternoon?"

"That is kind of you, and I should certainly enjoy it, but we live in opposite directions, sir. It would take you above three hours merely to reach my home."

"I should not regard it," Mr. Eversleigh declared. "Indeed, I would consider it a privilege. That is—if you are not already affianced? I do not mean to pry, Miss Stafford, but I cannot help noticing that dark-haired fellow over by the wall. He has been glowering at me for the past few moments, and since I am not acquainted with him, I can only think it because I have the honor of your company."

Candace knew without looking that he referred to Mr. Croyden. She, too, had been conscious of his steady regard, and wondered at the cause. It would almost appear that he was jealous, which, of course, was ridiculous, but she couldn't quite suppress the small surge of pleasure that shot through her at the notion.

Aware that she was behaving foolishly, Candace blushed, and did not dare look in Edward Croyden's direction. She raised her eyes to meet Mr. Eversleigh's gaze, but his attention had already wandered. So much for being an enchantress, she thought wryly, and turned to see what had captured her escort's attention.

An elderly woman, swathed in layers of green satin, sailed majestically across the ballroom floor. Diamonds glittered in her heavily powdered hair, at her ears, on her massive bosom and bejeweled fingers. Her head tilted imperiously high, she glanced neither to the right or left, but proceeded directly to the chair at the head of the room.

She was accompanied by a young man who paled in comparison to her magnificence, and a slender woman of indeterminate age and unremarkable features, neither of whom took any notice of the dozens of curious eyes watching their progress. Mr. Halbert, who normally might be expected to censure such a tardy arrival, greeted the old lady deferentially, and after assisting her into her chair, stood talking for several moments.

"Who is she?" Candace asked curiously.

Mr. Eversleigh, who, like everyone else in the ballroom, had stopped to observe the elderly woman's arrival, turned to his companion with a smile. "That, my dear Miss Stafford, is Lady Olivia Paxton, Countess of Hastings. She is considered the grand dame of Heptonstall Society, and is the founding patroness of our assembly rooms."

"She appears rather pretentious," Candace murmured, watching the way Lady Hastings held court, and the servile attitude of those who dared to approach her.

"Lady Hastings is the grandniece of the Duke of Buckingham, and a distant cousin, on her mother's side, to the queen. She knows everyone of any importance. Would you care to be presented?"

Candace shook her head. "Thank you, but no. I should not know what to say to her. Who is the other lady?"

"Mrs. Alicia Waldhauser—I believe she is a cousin of some sort, and resides with Lady Hastings. The young man is her nephew, Robert Paxton. Rumor has it that he is penniless and clings to her skirts in hopes of inheriting her fortune one day."

"Is it likely?"

Eversleigh shrugged. "She has no other kin, but I have heard she often declares her intention of leaving everything to her companion, Mrs. Waldhauser. The threat is sufficient to keep Mr. Paxton dancing attendance on her."

"How sad," Candace murmured. Her attention was caught as Robert Paxton, after listening intently to his aunt, scurried across the floor to speak to Edward Croyden.

"It appears your friend has been signally honored," Eversleigh commented. "Rarely does Lady Hastings condescend to acknowledge anyone's presence."

"Mr. Croyden is always full of surprises," Candace replied, but she, too, was intrigued that the elderly doyenne seemed to know him. She watched the unlikely pair converse for a moment, then noticed her aunt Emily gazing about inquisitively. She gazed up at Mr. Eversleigh. "Thank you, sir, for providing me a much-needed respite, but I believe my aunt is looking for me."

He immediately offered her his arm, and escorted her across the room. Candace presented him, but

174

her aunt was clearly distracted, and after a moment Mr. Eversleigh took his leave.

"What is it, Aunt Emily," Candace asked. "You seem worried."

A frown marring her brow, Emily confided in her niece. "I cannot find Thomasina. She was dancing with that nice Mr. Tyler, and then she suddenly disappeared. Have you seen her anywhere?"

"Perhaps she has gone to the retiring room," Candace suggested. While she had noticed Thomasina on the dance floor earlier, she realized it had been some time since she'd seen her elder cousin. Thomasina was an incurable flirt, but surely she would not wander off with any gentleman. . . .

"Would you see if you can find her, dear? Perhaps I am overly anxious, but I do not like her out of sight for so long."

Candace agreed and, after a few reassuring words to her aunt, made her way to the retiring room discreetly located in the hall outside the ballroom. Several young ladies occupied the various sofas and chairs placed there for their convenience, and used the privacy to repair torn gowns or fix wayward coiffures. Soft, feminine voices filled the air with lighthearted chatter and laughter, but Thomasina's was not among them. The only other place her cousin could be was on the balcony.

Candace had noticed the tall windows standing open to catch the breeze, and she had observed several young ladies slipping outside with their escorts. They risked their reputations by doing so, and Aunt Emily would certainly not approve of such permissive behavior. But Thomasina had become impatient of late with the rules governing one's conduct. Candace would not put it past her to stroll outside for a breath of air—and the opportunity to indulge in a minor flirtation.

After returning to the ballroom and making certain that her cousin had not also returned, Candace quietly edged toward the first set of open windows. The length of panes reached from the ceiling to the floor and swung outward toward the balcony. The cooling breeze swept in, and the stars beyond beckoned.

She glanced around, then casually stepped outside. It took a few moments for her eyes to adjust to the near darkness, but then she was able to discern several couples standing indecently close. To be out there, alone with a gentleman, and held in an intimate embrace, was undoubtedly improper. Just for a moment, however, she gazed wistfully at the couples.

The night was balmy, with a soft breeze blowing to cool flushed cheeks and impassioned hearts. A night made for romance, she thought, and almost felt envious of the young ladies willing to risk their reputation for the seductive promise of a kiss beneath the quarter moon. Candace drew a deep breath, reminding herself that she was there to search for her cousin. Unfortunately, the pale moonlight was insufficient to tell if Thomasina was among the couples scattered down the length of the terrace.

Candace hesitated, listening to the sounds of an occasional giggle, and a light admonishment to a gentleman to behave.

"May I be of assistance?"

She whirled at the sound of the deep voice behind her. Edward Croyden loomed distressingly near. Though she had done nothing wrong, Candace felt her cheeks flame and found it suddenly difficult to breathe normally.

"You seem to make a habit of wandering about alone, Miss Stafford, but do you think it wise?" he asked softly, his voice creating a whisper of warm air against her brow.

"I was looking for Thomasina," she managed to say as she gazed up at him. His broad shoulders blocked the light from the ballroom, and his eyes seemed like pools of inky blackness. Impossible to tell what he was thinking.

"Then allow me to escort you," he replied, and without waiting for her ascent he caught her hand and drew it through the bend of his arm.

Feeling the steel strength of his muscles through the sleeve of his coat, she thought it far more dangerous to be out there with him than alone. His touch ignited a sudden rush of warmth that radiated through her with the quickness of heat lightning. Her own muscles seemed to melt beneath his touch, and she was silently thankful for the support of his arm.

Seeking to break the spell he cast over her, Candace murmured, "I may be mistaken. I did not see her come out—"

"I did, about a quarter hour past," he interrupted, his low voice close to her ears. "She was with that blond fellow who partnered her in the quadrille. Shall we stroll toward the far corner? I believe I see them."

"Your eyesight is remarkable, sir. I can see nothing beyond my nose in this darkness."

"Perhaps I have had more experience than you," he teased.

His voice sent deliciously wicked shivers down

her back. How many ladies had he dallied with in the moonlight, she wondered. How many had he kissed beneath the stars? As her eyes became accustomed to the darkness, she glanced up at his handsome profile, and the strong line of his jaw. A reckless yearning grew inside her to know what it would be like to be kissed by him, to be held captive by those strong arms. . . .

"La, sir, I should not dare."

Candace stiffened as she heard her cousin's voice, followed by a girlish trill of laughter. Beside her, Mr. Croyden paused.

"I believe that sounds like your cousin," he whispered, a rumble of amusement underlining his words.

Embarrassed, Candace released his arm and stepped toward the couple at the far end of the balcony. "Thomasina? Aunt Emily is searching everywhere for you. You must go in at once."

For a moment there was silence, then a rustle of silk. A second later Thomasina emerged into a small pool of candlelight that reflected from one of the windows. Two of her long curls had come unpinned, and her eyes shown unnaturally bright. She glared at her cousin. "Is that you, Candace? Gracious, I only stepped out for a breath of air. There was no need for you to come searching for me."

"I fear Aunt Emily does not share your opinion," Candace retorted, vexed at her cousin's air of annoyance. "She is extremely worried, and if you do not care for her concern, you should think of your own reputation. Really—"

"Heavens, spare me the sermon. You sound more like Papa every day," Thomasina interrupted with a forced laugh. She turned to the young man who had accompanied her, and placed her hand on his arm. "Pray excuse my cousin, sir. I fear she is very provincial. Will you escort me in? 'Tis certain we shall have no peace out here."

Shocked and a little hurt, Candace watched her cousin walk away. The other couples, who had undoubtedly heard the argument, hastily followed Thomasina inside. Mortified, Candace drew a deep breath and turned to Croyden. "I . . . I don't know what possessed Thomasina to behave so . . ."

"Brazenly?" Croyden asked with a chuckle. "The little minx deserves to be spanked, but do not be too hard on her. Moonlight can be intoxicating. I can understand how she might be tempted to allow the gentleman a kiss."

"Well, I cannot," Candace declared, and started toward the windows.

"Can you not?" Croyden asked softly. He captured her hand and drew her close to him.

She felt his strong arm encircling her waist, and his other hand rested beneath her chin, tilting her face up so that she gazed into his smoky eyes. Her heart beating erratically, she felt powerless to move.

"I have been very good, Miss Stafford, but you would tempt a saint. Do you know how beautiful your eyes look in the moonlight?"

His head bent toward her. She knew she was about to be kissed, and though the more prudent part of her soul warned her she should not allow it, the rest of her longed for the experience. She closed her eyes and lifted her chin.

His lips grazed her cheek with a feathery softness, then teased the corner of her mouth. She felt his arm tighten about her waist, drawing her closer. Candace unconsciously lifted her arms to encircle his neck.

"Bewitching," he murmured just before his mouth claimed hers. He kissed her gently at first, and though he held her securely, he was ready to release her the instant she protested. Instead, she surprised him with the sweetness of her lips, returning his kiss with a generosity that sent the fire surging through him. He deepened the kiss, tumbling them both into a world neither had dreamed of.

Candace pressed against him, yearning to be as close as possible, thrilling to the waves of pleasure his kisses evoked. When he pulled back, she slowly opened her eyes and gazed up at him.

Innocence, wonder, and desire battled for dominance in her silvery eyes, and Damian groaned. "Don't look at me like that, my sweet."

"Like what?" she asked, knowing she should pull away, knowing she should protest, but wanting only to prolong the moment.

"Like a temptress," he told her, and tried to ease the desire he felt by lightly kissing the tip of her nose. "Come, Miss Stafford, I think I had best escort you inside. I warned you it was dangerous out here."

She breathed deeply, trying to still her racing pulse. "I believe you said . . . it was dangerous alone."

"So I did, but I have discovered you go to my head like fine wine." His fingers gently caressed a curl near her cheek. "I could very easily forget I am a gentleman."

"And if you did?" she heard herself asking wistfully. She was shocked at her own conduct, but still reluctant to leave the warmth of his arms and the magnetic pull of his smoky eyes. He awakened feelings in her she'd not known she possessed, delicious, wonderful feelings that made her heart beat faster and set her senses reeling.

He deliberately captured her hands and turned her to face the door. "Do not tempt me too far, Candace," he warned, his breath warm on her neck. "One day we shall finish what we started here, but this is neither the time nor the place."

She had to be content with that, but her steps were slow as they strolled back along the terrace. She was reluctant to face him in the glittering light of the ballroom.

"Will you save the last dance for me," he whispered softly as they stepped into the ballroom.

She nodded but could not look at him. Her eyes scanned the ballroom, but no one seemed to have noticed their absence. The same young ladies pirouetted on the dance floor, and the same young men bowed gracefully in response beneath a hundred blazing candles. She wondered how everything could look precisely the same when she felt so different inside.

"Excuse me," Robert Paxton apologized as he approached them. "I regret the intrusion, Lord Doncaster, but my aunt would like another word with you."

Candace glanced up at Croyden and saw the consternation in his eyes. "Lord Doncaster?" she whispered.

"Oh, dear, have I given your secret away?" Paxton asked. "I do apologize, my lord. I know you wished to travel incognito, but I assumed the young lady knew your true identity."

Candace barely heard him. She withdrew her

arm from Croyden and turned to Mr. Paxton. "Would you be so good, sir, as to escort me to my aunt?"

"Candace, allow me to explain—"

"I do not believe there is anything more to be said, *my lord*. I suggest you do not keep Lady Hastings waiting."

Chapter 12

Emily observed her niece as she entered the breakfast room early Thursday morning, noting with disapproval that Candace was dressed for riding in her old habit, the blue color sadly faded and the jacket mended in several places. Her hair was swept back into a severe bun again so that she hardly looked like the same lovely girl who had graced the dance floor the night before.

Emily took a sip of her tea before asking tactfully, "Surely, you are not going riding? Did I not mention that Mr. Croyden promised to call?"

Candace fussed with the dishes on the sideboard, avoiding her aunt's eyes. "I promised Mrs. Bellweather I would look in on her this morning."

"That is very commendable of you, darling, but can your visit not wait until later? I know Mr. Croyden will be most disappointed if he calls and finds you not at home."

Candace carried her plate to the breakfast table and sat down at the opposite end. She was tempted to tell her aunt that she had no desire to see Mr. Croyden ever again—and that Croyden was not even his name. Lord Doncaster, Mr. Paxton had called him. Thinking of how basely she had been deceived, Candace burned with anger.

She was furious with him and furious with herself for caring. And she had allowed herself to care even more than she was willing to admit. Bluedeviled, Candace sighed. If only she had known his true identity—she would have taken precautions to keep her distance. And Uncle Jonathan would never have allowed him to run free in the vicarage. It was one thing to allow plain "Mr. Croyden" to stand on terms with his family, but her uncle would not have extended such hospitality to a member of the peerage. His aversion to the nobility ran even deeper than Candace's.

"Did you hear me, my dear?" her aunt asked, intruding on her thoughts.

"I am sorry, Aunt Emily. I fear I did not get sufficient sleep, and my mind is wandering this morning."

"Well, that is not surprising, considering how late we arrived home. Indeed, I am astonished to see you down so early—are your cousins still abed?"

Candace nodded as she took a bite of the eggs. She had no appetite, but knew if she did not at least make a pretense of eating, her aunt would insist on giving her a restorative.

"I thought I would allow all of you to sleep late. Gracious, I believe you girls danced nearly every set, so 'tis little wonder if you are a trifle tired." When Candace did not comment, she continued. "I am so thankful Mr. Croyden suggested the evening. The benefit of the experience will stand all of you in good stead when we go to London. I only hope he will offer to escort us again."

"I doubt he will remain in the village for long," Candace replied. "I believe he said something about needing to return to his estate."

"That is disappointing, but I suppose we must be thankful for the time Mr. Croyden has spared us. Such an obliging gentleman—we owe him a great deal."

Candace bit her lip to keep from responding that they owed him nothing. Mr. Croyden had befriended them for his own nefarious reasons. She didn't know precisely what those reasons were, but it galled her that her aunt considered herself in his debt. Shoving her dish away, Candace rose. "Pray excuse me, Aunt Emily."

"My dear, I do wish you would not go out this morning. What am I to say to Mr. Croyden? He particularly asked that I tell you he intended to call."

"It is regrettable he did not tell me personally, since I had made other plans, but I suppose gentlemen of his nature always expect others to accommodate their whims."

"Gentlemen of his nature?" Emily repeated, gazing at her in astonishment. She carefully set down her cup. "Candace, what has Mr. Croyden done to offend you? Have you quarreled with him? Is that why you insisted on riding home with Theresa last night instead of coming with us in his carriage?"

"We did not quarrel, precisely," Candace murmured, already regretting her hasty words. "I just . . . I dislike the way he assumes everyone will rush to do his bidding." She had considered confessing the truth to her aunt and uncle, but it would mean revealing her involvement with Harry, which would not only ruin her reputation, but hurt her aunt and uncle deeply. It might still come to that, but she hoped Lord Doncaster would simply leave, and no one need ever know how foolishly she had behaved.

Emily stared at her niece. She had been very nearly certain that Candace, if not actually in love with Croyden, at least harbored a warm *tendre* for him. Something was dreadfully wrong. But before she could question her niece further, Theresa and Thomasina, chattering and giggling, and full of high spirits, stepped into the room and wished her a good morning. After greeting her daughters, Emily looked around for her niece, but she had quietly slipped out the door.

Candace had studiously avoided Lord Doncaster the evening before, even, as her aunt had suggested, exchanging places with Thomasina so that she would not be forced to make polite conversation with him in the carriage during the drive home. It had been all she could manage to thank him civilly before saying good night.

She told herself she had no desire to see him, or speak to him ever again. But she could not quite suppress the urge to talk about him—and the only person she could safely do so with was Mrs. Bellweather.

She found the elderly woman ensconced as usual in her chair by the window, and apologized for intruding on her so early in the morning.

"Nonsense, child. I have been up for hours, and, it appears, I am not alone." She nodded toward the window. "There goes Jasper Fairgood and his mother. Have you made up your quarrel with him?"

"Not really, although we are polite to each other," Candace replied, rising to glance out the window. There was no mistaking Jasper's lumbering, ancient town carriage. "I wonder where they can be going."

"I can think of no other destination than the vicarage, but that is hardly likely if you have not made up your quarrel—unless, of course, he wishes to apologize for his behavior."

Candace watched the carriage until it disappeared from sight, a sense of unease settling over her. She sank into the chair opposite Mrs. Bellweather and accepted a cup of tea thankfully. "I cannot imagine Jasper apologizing, and certainly not with his mother along."

"Well, do not let it trouble you," the older woman advised with a smile. "Part of the charm of living in a village like Thatchwood is that nothing remains secret for long. Of course, that is also one of the disadvantages. Now, tell me what brings you out so early. Did you attend the assembly last evening?"

Knowing Mrs. Bellweather would enjoy hearing all the details, Candace described the ballroom vividly, and painted a glowing word picture of the gowns the ladies had worn and the glittering attire of the gentlemen in attendance. She described the dances, the musicians, and even the chaperons flawlessly, but her voice faltered as she mentioned the entrance of Lady Hastings.

"I know her," Mrs. Bellweather commented, "and there is not a more opinionated, pretentious woman in all England. Was Alicia Waldhauser with her?"

"I believe that was the name of her companion—a rather slender woman with auburn hair?"

"Amazing. I cannot believe she is still with Olivia after all these years. I knew Alicia when she was a girl, and a sweeter, more gentle-hearted person would be hard to find. She was widowed very young and, as she was some sort of distant relation, packed off to live with Olivia. I thought it a great pity at the time, but Alicia's husband had left her penniless, so she had little choice. Had it been me, I doubtless would have strangled Olivia by now. Were you presented to her ladyship?"

Candace shook her head.

"Consider yourself fortunate. She has illusions of grandeur—fancies herself royalty. Well, child, if she did not disturb you, what did? Something happened to put those shadows in your pretty eyes."

Candace smiled wanly. Her hands cradled her teacup for warmth while she sought to put her feelings into words. After a moment she looked up at her companion and explained haltingly, "Mr. Croyden had spoken with Lady Hastings earlier—she apparently knew him from London—"

"She makes it a point to know anyone worth knowing."

"I had just come in from the balcony with him," Candace continued, then blushed under Maude Bellweather's knowing gaze. "Aunt Emily sent us to look for Thomasina," she added hastily, and saw no reason to mention that she had so far forgot herself as to allow Mr. Croyden to kiss her. . . .

"Go on, child," Mrs. Bellweather prompted.

"Lady Hastings saw us and sent her nephew across to ask Mr. Croyden to attend her, only Mr. Paxton . . . addressed him as Lord Doncaster."

"Oh, dear, let the cat out of the bag, did she? One never could trust Olivia Paxton to keep a secret."

"You knew?" Candace asked with a look of hurt betrayal.

Mrs. Bellweather sighed. She leaned forward and patted Candace on the shoulder. "I suspected as much when you first told me about him. Croyden is a family name, and when you mentioned his estate was called Deerpark, I assumed he must be related, but I was not certain until I saw him. I knew his father rather well, and your young man is the image of him."

"He is not my young man," Candace snapped, her nerves frayed. "And I do wish you had told me the truth about him."

"Why, child?" Maude asked gently.

"Why? Because I . . . I would have avoided him." She set down her cup and rose, pacing the room restlessly. "Good heavens, can you not see the position I am in? He is a member of the aristocracy. I do not know his rank but—"

"Damian inherited his father's title. He is the Earl of Doncaster."

"Damian? Is that his true name?" Candace demanded, whirling around. But even as she asked the question, she knew it was true. The name suited him perfectly.

"Damian Edward Croyden Reynald," the old woman said softly. "He did not deceive you entirely."

But Candace was not listening. She had heard only the *Reynald* and the pieces of the puzzle fell into place with blinding clarity. "Oh, no. Then he really is Harry's brother?"

"Did he not tell you so?" Maude asked, her eyes twinkling.

"He did, but in such a manner that he knew I would not believe him. Oh, the wretch! The despicable, duplicitous wretch!" She sank into the chair and leaned back, closing her eyes. But a second later they flew open again. "And Harry—that abominable boy! That is why he was so astonished when I thought Mr. Croyden—Lord Doncaster—meant him harm. But if they are brothers, then why did not Harry turn to him for help? Oh, I do not understand any of this."

"Doncaster told me he'd had a falling-out with his brother. Harry had, as the result of a silly wager, somehow managed to accidentally set fire to their neighbor's barn. It was not the first time the boy had been in trouble, only this time Doncaster refused to stand the nonsense. Harry apparently left Deerpark in a huff, vowing to pay off the debt himself."

Candace rubbed her aching head. "He told me something of the sort, that he had debts which he must make good, and he was determined to do so without turning to his family for help . . . but Harry feared someone was trying to kill him—surely he could not have suspected his brother?"

"No, but 'tis the reason Doncaster was not using his title. He, too, knew someone had ambushed Harry and thought it wisest not to let anyone know of his own presence here. Would you care for more tea, my dear?"

Candace held out her cup and allowed the older woman to refill it. She still found it difficult to believe that Mrs. Bellweather had known the earl's true identity all this time and never breathed a word, and she very much resented that Croyden—Lord Doncaster—Damian, whatever his name was, had not confided in her. She took a sip of the tea and repeated peevishly, "I do wish you had told me the truth about Doncaster."

"It was not my secret to divulge," Mrs. Bellweather replied with unruffled composure. "Candace, my child, you are behaving foolishly. Gracious, to hear you talk one would think Doncaster was a three-eyed monster with a horn growing out of his head. There is no law that states a member of the aristocracy cannot court you."

She flushed beneath the rebuke, but lifted her chin stubbornly. "Are you not forgetting my mother?"

"Not at all, but I wish you would contrive to do so. Candace, my dear, the cases are very different. For one thing, you are not married."

"No, nor likely to be."

"I rather think you underestimate Doncaster, my dear. He has been assiduous in his attentions to you, and I do not believe it was merely because of his brother. Nor do I believe you to be entirely indifferent to him."

Candace shook her head. "I fear the world will not share your opinion, Mrs. Bellweather. And no matter my own feelings, Lord Doncaster will not be seeking to wed the penniless niece of a village vicar, with a scandal attached to her name. It would be a dreadful misalliance."

"I suggest you leave that to Lord Doncaster to decide."

Candace set down her cup and rose to take her leave. Maude Bellweather was a dear, sweet soul, but she had obviously been isolated in her tiny cottage for so long that she had forgotten the ways of the world. It was only in plays that the wealthy lord married the poor waif.

Candace allowed Garnet to meander along at her own slow pace. She was in no hurry to return to the vicarage, and Mrs. Bellweather had given her much to think about. But she had not gone far when the sound of a carriage caught her attention. She glanced behind her and saw the yellow curricle Mr. Croyden drove fast approaching.

Knowing there was no hope of outriding the gentleman, Candace reluctantly drew Garnet to the side of the road. She hoped he would have the civility to merely drive past, but he reined in alongside of her.

"Good day, Miss Stafford," he said with that engaging grin that made her heart beat faster than it was ever meant to.

"My lord," she responded, trying to sound composed as she observed him from beneath the wide brim of her bonnet. He looked disgustingly handsome—and well rested. If he had spent a troubled night, there was no sign of it in his clear eyes, or in his immaculate attire. Conscious of her own shabby dress, she wished again that he would just go away.

Damian, however, had other intentions. "If you are riding to the vicarage, I will bear you company. I think we have much to discuss."

"On the contrary, my lord, I have naught to say to you, and no wish for your company."

He winced. "I once thought that nothing could sound worse on your lips than the way you say *Mr. Croyden* so contemptuously. But I was wrong. You somehow manage to make 'my lord' sound insulting."

Candace turned her mare, trying very hard to ignore the warmth of his smoky eyes and the enticing curve of his mouth. Her pulse fluttered as she recalled how his lips had felt against hers. Repressing a strong urge to repeat the experience, she glared at him. "Perhaps you have yet another name or title you would prefer I use?"

"I would prefer you do not judge me until you give me a chance to explain."

"I have heard enough of your explanations, my lord. Pray excuse me," she retorted, and nudged Garnet. The mare stubbornly refused to move. For all Candace's efforts, Garnet's hooves might have been nailed to the ground.

Damian laughed aloud. "At least your mare is willing to listen. Candace, do be reasonable. We must talk—I have just come from seeing your uncle."

"Really? And under what guise did you present yourself? Mr. Croyden, Damian Reynald, or the Earl of Doncaster?" She nudged the mare again with her boot, muttering beneath her breath, "Do move, Garnet."

Damian looped the reins of his own team, tied them securely, and climbed down from his curricle. He approached her with a determined light in his eyes.

"What . . . what are you doing?"

"Simply attempting to bring you to your senses, my sweet. I had hoped to wait until this trouble with Harry was settled, but I can see that is no longer possible." He took advantage of her astonishment to remove the reins from her hands, and before she could protest, he was leading Garnet, the traitorous beast, to the rear of his curricle.

Recovering her wits, she railed at him, "Your conduct is outrageous, sir. Take your hands off my horse at once."

"Certainly." He tied the mare's reins to the back of his carriage, then turned to face her. His dark eyes crinkled with amusement. "I can think of several places I would much rather place my hands."

"Stay away from me," she warned, brandishing her riding crop as he approached.

"Impossible," he murmured. He deftly caught hold of her wrist, and the crop dropped from her suddenly nerveless fingers. His hands went around her waist, and he stood there for a second, gazing into her green eyes. "Even with your hair in that torturous bun, you look enchantingly beautiful."

Candace hardened her heart against his flattery. "Have you and your brother not done sufficient damage to my reputation? Must you accost me on a public road?"

Damian glanced around. There was not a carriage or horse to be seen in either direction. "I think you are safe for the moment," he said as he lifted her down from Garnet's back and into his arms.

He settled her against him, cradling her securely with one of his arms beneath her shoulders and the other under her knees. In that instance Candace knew she had inherited her mother's passion. It was unquestionably, indecently, wicked to allow a man to hold her in such an intimate embrace, but she could not help the shivers of delight that danced down her spine. Waves of desire cascaded through her until her blood tingled and her pulses pounded with an inexplicable yearning to be held even closer.

Candace knew she must fight against her own urges, but when Damian lowered his head toward her, she merely closed her eyes. Even then she could not shut him out. She felt a feather-light kiss against her brow, and the whisper softness of his breath as his lips brushed a sensitive spot just below her ear.

"You can open your eyes now," Damian said as he sat her on the seat of the curricle. "I will drive you home—if that is what you wish."

She blinked into the brilliant sunlight, momentarily missing the warmth of his embrace. Then she came to her senses. As Damian circled around to the far side of the carriage, she scrambled down. "I am not going anywhere with you, my lord."

"You think not?" he asked, immediately reversing his steps.

She dodged around the horses and eyed him warily across their backs, her breath coming in ragged gasps.

"Candace, I wish only to talk to you. Darling, must we play tag in the middle of the road?"

Darling. The natural way he said the word turned her bones to jelly. Concentrate, she told herself. Imagine the scandal. But all she could think of was how easy it would be to allow him to catch her. He'd probably pick her up again, perhaps kiss her . . . she must not think of such things. Edging her way down the side of the carriage, Candace begged, "Please, just go away, Mr. Croyden—"

"Damian," he corrected her, grinning wickedly.

"Whatever," she retorted, exasperated. "You are as irresponsible as Harry—"

"Oh? Are you finally admitting you met my brother?"

"I should have realized at once that you were related. Insanity obviously runs in your family."

"I will own I am crazy about you—blast it, Candace, stand still. We cannot converse in this manner."

"I told you I have nothing to say to you," she said as she reached the rear of the carriage. She could easily reach up and untie her reins, but Garnet would be of little help. Damian could walk faster than her old mare could run. She wondered fleetingly if she could climb back into the curricle and drive off with his team. On the off chance that it might be possible, she unloosed Garnet's reins.

"You will not escape me on that nag," Damian warned as he approached on the other side of the curricle.

She dropped the reins, knowing there was no danger of Garnet wandering off. Hoping he would think she'd merely realized the futility of her effort, she raced along the side of the carriage. Would he come around Garnet after her? It was her only hope.

As if realizing her intent, Damian remained on the left side of the carriage, matching his steps to hers. Unfortunately, he was much closer to his horse's reins than she was.

"You give new meaning to the phrase 'chasing after a lady,' but you are not in an enviable position, my dear. I did warn you, riding out alone was dangerous."

"Not until you began frequenting the neighborhood—"

"Either get in the carriage or mount Garnet," he interrupted abruptly.

"I will not be ordered about by you, my lord—"

"Very well, my sweet. If you wish to be observed cavorting on a country lane, remain where you are. I am sure you will afford considerable entertainment to whoever is driving that carriage."

Startled, Candace glanced toward the south. She could barely see the approaching carriage, but judging by the cloud of dust the horses kicked up, it was traveling rapidly. She hastily climbed into the curricle as Damian mounted from the other side.

"That is better," he said with satisfaction as he grabbed the reins and gently urged his team to a trot. "I suppose Garnet can be trusted to trail along after us?"

"She will certainly head for the stable," Candace murmured, "but I hope that as soon as this carriage passes, you will set me down."

"You may get your wish," Damian muttered, his eyes narrowing as he studied the approaching town coach.

The carriage swept by them in a blur of dust and pounding hooves. Candace had a quick glimpse of an elaborately gilded coach with an ornate crest on the door panel. Four perfectly matched horses, all a beautiful chestnut brown, pulled the equipage.

Damian drew his team to a halt a moment later and glanced around to make certain Garnet was not far behind. The old mare grazed placidly alongside the road, almost precisely where they'd left her.

He turned back to Candace and smiled. "I fear we must continue this fascinating conversation later, my dear. Will you forgive me if I leave you to ride to the vicarage alone?"

"Forgive you?" she repeated, stunned. "Why, I have been requesting that you do so this past half hour, and furthermore—"

Holding the reins in one hand, he reached around her with the other and pulled her close. His lips effectively stopped her tirade by claiming her mouth in a warm, if brief, kiss. He drew back after a second, kissed the tip of her nose, and then re-

197

leased her. "I am sorry, my sweet, but the gentleman in that carriage is the Duke of Cardiff."

Confused and shaken, Candace gazed up at him. "A friend of yours, my lord?"

"I rather think he came to see Harry, but if you will excuse me, I shall see if I cannot make him feel welcome."

Chapter 13

Harry Reynald, having made excellent time, arrived in Lower Thatchwood on Thursday. His arm was on the mend, he was clean shaven, and neatly attired in a tight-fitting riding coat of blue superfine and buff pantaloons. All in all, he looked very different from the pale boy in tattered clothes Candace had befriended. He whistled a tune as he cantered down High Street.

As he reached the bridge leading to Upper Thatchwood, Harry reined in Majestic and took a moment to gaze fondly at the pastoral scene before him. The woods, where he had spent so much time, banked the road on the right, and still, he hoped, harbored their secrets.

He had half expected to encounter Candace, but he had seen no sign of the old mare she habitually rode, or the dilapidated pony cart she sometimes used, at the few houses he'd passed. He knew from Candace which was the vicarage and had lingered on the hill above for a few moments, observing the long drive and tidy yard, hoping for a glimpse of her. His vigil was rewarded only by the arrival of an antiquated black carriage, and though it was impossible to be certain from a distance, he thought he recognized Mr. Fairgood as the gentleman who accompanied an elderly lady into the house.

Harry couldn't help grinning as he recalled their previous encounter. Jasper Fairgood seemed as pompous and antiquated as the lumbering carriage he drove, but Harry had shook him to the soles of his Wellingtons and could not be sorry for it. The man was a fool if he thought Candace would ever betray anyone she had given her loyalty to. She was too good for him, in Harry's opinion, but Candace obviously liked the fellow.

Harry watched for a moment longer, shook his head at the capriciousness of women, then nudged his horse. He knew from his explorations that he had merely to continue along High Street, and the dusty road would lead him to the Boar's Head Inn, where Damian had been staying.

Harry hoped his brother was still there—it would give him a great deal of pleasure to inform Damian that his assistance was not needed. He smiled, thinking of the heavy purse tucked in his saddle-bags. Old Bideford had cut up handsomely when Harry told him his string of hunters was for sale. He now had sufficient money to pay Cardiff what he owed, restore their neighbor's barn, and redeem his father's ring. And there would even be enough left to reward Candace for her assistance.

The last would be tricky. He had to be careful not to let on that he had met the young lady previously, especially if she'd patched up her quarrel with Fairgood. But he had thought of a way it might be arranged. If Damian was still at the inn, then naturally he would wish to introduce his younger brother to the Trents. After that it would be only a matter of time before Harry managed a few minutes alone with Candace.

Satisfied with the way events were progressing, he walked his stallion across the bridge, then scanned the surrounding woods. Not a sign of life. It appeared the pair who had trailed him across England had finally given up the chase. He'd not had sight nor sound of them since leaving the village.

It was deuced odd, he thought, and had they not inquired about him by name, he would be inclined to think it was a case of mistaken identity. But they had asked for him at various inns, and they had deliberately laid in wait for him. Harry had overheard part of their conversation—enough to convince him that the pair of rapscallions intended to put an end to his life. Yet, now the men seemed to have disappeared, and he still had no clue as to who they were, or what he had done to offend someone so dreadfully that such drastic measures were employed.

He might never know the truth of it, Harry realized, which was a very unsatisfactory state of affairs. Perhaps when he returned to London, he would call in at Bow Street. Maybe the Runners could discover something. He would ask Damian's advice.

Chuckling aloud at the thought of his brother's astonishment were he to make such a request, Harry set Majestic to a canter. In the past Damian had freely given his advice, which, more often than not, had been ignored. This would be the first time Harry had voluntarily sought his big brother's counsel. Imagining Damian's shock, Harry picked up the pace. Surprisingly, he discovered he was almost eager to see Damian again.

Emily Trent, seated in the sewing room at the vicarage, looked up from her needlepoint. "Yes, Mary, what is it?"

"Beg pardon, Mrs. Trent, but Mrs. Fairgood is here with Mr. Fairgood, and asking to see you and the vicar."

"Is she, indeed? Show her into the drawing room and tell her I shall be with her directly," Emily ordered, and laid aside her sewing. Although Jonathan had warned her not to discuss the very startling news he had told her that morning, even forbidding her to confide in her daughters, she hoped Maria Fairgood had somehow heard the delicious tidbit. Emily would positively delight in telling her it was true.

She directed her daughters to continue with their sewing, tidied her hair, adjusted the ruffles at her throat, and then proceeded slowly to the drawing room.

Jasper rose at once as she entered. He looked unnaturally pale and ill at ease, but Emily hardly noticed. Her gaze was drawn to young Darby, the lad who did the gardening for Mrs. Bellweather. He squirmed beneath the firm grip Maria had on his shoulder, and perspiration beaded his brow. Was the boy in some sort of trouble?

"Good day, Emily," Maria said pleasantly. "I pray you will forgive this intrusion, but a rather serious matter has come to my attention, one which, I am sad to say, concerns a member of your family. Although it grieves me deeply to be the bearer of such news, I know you will agree that it is my Christian duty to come forward." She glanced behind Emily. "Is our good reverend not at home?"

"He is in the library," Emily admitted, "but he is working on his sermon and hates to be disturbed. Perhaps if you would tell me—"

"I am certain the vicar will wish to hear what we have to say," Maria interrupted. "This matter is of the gravest importance. If necessary, we shall wait until he is available."

Feeling thoroughly confused, Emily gestured toward the chairs. "Please be seated, then, and I shall see if Mr. Trent will join us." She pulled the bell rope and, when Mary appeared, instructed the girl to inform Mr. Trent that his presence was required in the drawing room. While they waited, she politely offered tea, but her guests declined any refreshments and the uncomfortable silence in the room continued unabated.

After a few moments Emily attempted to make polite conversation, but her comments were answered with monosyllabic replies, and she finally gave up the effort. She looked up in relief when Jonathan entered the room.

"I regret interrupting you, sir, but Mrs. Fairgood insisted that you attend us. She has distressing news, which, she says, concerns a member of our family."

"I see," he said, glancing with raised brows in Maria's direction, which caused his heavy spectacles to slide down his nose. "Very well, then, but I hope you will be brief."

Maria's bosom swelled. "I assure you, my good sir, that I do not come before you lightly, and only the high regard in which I hold your family would persuade me to undertake what I can term as only a most unpleasant task."

Jonathan sighed. His calling required him to be patient and tactful, but both commodities were in short supply that morning. Edward Croyden, whom he must now learn to address as Lord Doncaster, had visited him at the church earlier, and the revelations that gentleman laid before him still rankled. He had barely had time to consider their conversation, when Mary announced Mrs. Fairgood wished to see him. Jonathan suspected she had somehow learned about his lordship, and it was that news she wished to announce.

He glanced at her impatiently. "Yes, well, I am certain we all appreciate your concern. However, if this concerns Mr. Croyden, you need not trouble yourself."

"Croyden?" Maria retorted disdainfully. "I know nothing of him, save that he is an encroaching mushroom lacking in manners and breeding. Indeed, I have been astonished that you receive him in your home so frequently. If you were to ask my advice, sir, I would recommend you sever the connection."

Jonathan glanced uneasily around. For the first time, he noticed young Darby and observed Jasper standing near the window, looking very much as though he wished he were elsewhere.

"I suggest you send for Miss Stafford," Maria continued gravely, her voice at odds with the gleam of anticipation in her small eyes.

"Candace is not at home," Emily said, and suddenly feeling the need to explain, added, "She rode over to visit with Mrs. Bellweather."

"Is that what she told you?" Maria asked scorn-

204

fully. "Perhaps when you hear what I have to say, you will heed my advice in the future. I did warn you that it was courting trouble to allow your girls to traipse about alone."

Emily, resentful of Maria's tone and manner, was about to retort, when Jonathan spoke.

"My dear Mrs. Fairgood, I have neither the time nor the inclination to listen to baseless innuendos. I gather that Candace has somehow managed to offend you. What, precisely, has she done?"

"I had hoped to break the news more gently, but if you wish plain speaking—very well. Your niece, sir, has been secretly meeting a man in Squire Epsom's woods!"

"Preposterous," Jonathan stated firmly. "I do not believe it."

"Nor do I," Emily said, rising to stand beside her husband. "From where did you hear such a nonsensical story?"

Jasper stepped forward. His sallow skin was unnaturally pale, and he tugged at his cravat, but he met Jonathan's gaze squarely. "It pains me to say so, sir, but I saw her with my own eyes. Apparently she had been meeting this man for some time in the gamekeeper's cottage."

"What man?" Emily demanded, bristling. "This is ridiculous. Jasper, I realize your pride must have been greatly wounded when Candace broke off your betrothal, but to concoct such a tale as this . . ." She shook her head sadly.

Maria laughed rudely. "My dear Emily, Jasper, being the gentleman that he is, *allowed* Miss Stafford to put it about that she had broken their engagement, but the truth is, he withdrew when he found her in a compromising situation."

205

"There never was any engagement—" Emily retorted, but Jonathan silenced her with a hand on her arm.

"Let us try to discuss this rationally. Mr. Fairgood, when and with whom did you see my niece?"

Jasper flushed. "I don't know the man's name— but it was the morning after our excursion to Heptonstall. I called here to make certain Candace had arrived safely home, but she had ridden out a few moments earlier—purportedly to visit Mrs. Bellweather. Naturally, I rode after her, and you may imagine my dismay, the shock I experienced, when I came across her in the woods—in the arms of another man."

"There must be some explanation," Jonathan said. "I simply will not believe my niece capable of such duplicity."

Maria nodded. "Your sentiments do you justice, sir. I assure you my own reaction was much the same, and it was with the utmost reluctance that I finally accepted the truth. Naturally, you will require some small measure of proof. I believe you will find what this lad has to say extraordinarily interesting." She nudged the gangly boy beside her, and he reluctantly stood. "You are, I believe, acquainted with young Darby. Of late, he has been employed by Mrs. Bellweather."

"We all know Darby," Jonathan said impatiently.

"Tell the vicar what you saw." Maria prodded the boy. "You need not be afraid."

Darby wasn't afraid, but he was uncomfortable and embarrassed. He stood with his head down, and his booted foot dug a hole in the carpet. He liked Miss Stafford and was reluctant to say anything that would cause her grief. However, Mrs.

Fairgood had told him that not only was it his Christian duty to report what he had seen, but if he did not cooperate, she would have him arrested for poaching.

"I seen the gent," he finally muttered.

"Saw who?" Jonathan asked gently.

"The man staying in the gamekeeper's hut. I seen him a few times when I was fishing in the squire's stream. Miss Stafford brought him some food, and she showed him how to make a fishing pole."

"Unfortunately, the cad has since decamped," Jasper informed them. "However, I searched the cottage, and there is every indication that someone has been staying there. I also found this," he said, and dramatically drew an embroidered linen handkerchief from his pocket.

Emily, recognizing Candace's handiwork, moaned faintly.

Jonathan helped his wife to a chair, then turned to the lad. "Tell me, Darby, did you ever hear Miss Stafford call this man by name?"

"Yes, sir. She called him Harry."

"More evidence of the intimacy between your niece and this rogue," Maria declared. "Addressing him in such an informal manner bespeaks a certain familiarity. One can only wonder how long she had been meeting him clandestinely."

Jonathan ignored her. "Thank you, Darby, for speaking so forthrightly. You may wait outside."

When the double doors were securely shut behind the boy, the vicar turned to Jasper and his mother. "I am deeply appreciative of your concern for Candace, and I hope that such concern will ensure that neither of you will speak of this . . . incident beyond this room."

"You need not fear that, sir." Jasper replied at once.

"Send the girl away," Maria advised. "Pack her off to some relative with instructions that she be properly chaperoned."

Jonathan looked at her for a moment, then spoke decisively. "I had foolishly hoped it would not be necessary to divulge what I was told in strictest confidence. It is with the utmost reluctance that I go back on my word, but I cannot allow my niece's reputation to be so unfairly blemished when she was only obeying my instructions."

"I am afraid I do not understand," Jasper said.

"You see, Candace has been acting as my emissary. The gentleman she carried food to, and helped to nurse back to health, is Harry Reynald, the younger brother of the Earl of Doncaster. It was I who gave him permission to stay in the gamekeeper's hut. The poor young man turned up at the church seeking a refuge after he had been ambushed. His shoulder was badly wounded, and Mr. Reynald feared for his life—which was why it was necessary to keep his presence here a secret. Not even Mrs. Trent knew that I had given him sanctuary."

Maria, her mouth hanging open, stared at him, dumbfounded. Jasper was shocked speechless, and Emily gazed at her husband with something akin to adoration.

Jonathan continued smoothly. "It was undoubtedly wrong of me to ask Candace to assist Mr. Reynald, but her habit of driving alone and visiting the ailing members of our congregation gave her the freedom to move about without arousing undue suspicion. Of course, once I was able to reach Lord Doncaster, he took matters into his own hands, and he assures me his brother is now quite safe."

Recovering her wits, Maria asked suspiciously, "Lord Doncaster, you say? Not that I doubt your word, sir, but I must think it odd that we have seen no strangers in the village, and certainly someone as distinguished as the Earl of Doncaster must be noticed."

Jonathan smiled sweetly. "How perceptive of you, Mrs. Fairgood, but his lordship, fearful for his brother's safety, did not wish to advertise his presence. He arrived here under an assumed name. Apparently, his disguise was most effective. I believe you were even introduced to the gentleman."

A look of absolute horror crossed her face. "Not . . . not Mr. Croyden!" she moaned. For the first time in her life, Maria Fairgood fainted.

Jasper retrieved his mother's smelling salts from her reticule, and Emily later brought Maria a reviving cup of tea, but even so, it was nearly an hour before she felt sufficiently recovered to allow her son to drive her home.

Emily could barely contain her impatience, and the moment the door shut behind their departing visitors, she turned to her husband. "I have never heard you tell so many taradiddles in all our lives together."

"I was inspired," he said, his round eyes gleaming with mischief. "And if it costs me my place in heaven, I vow it worth it, just to have seen the look on Maria Fairgood's face."

"For shame, sir," Emily said, but after glancing about the hall to make certain they were quite alone, she stepped close to her husband and kissed him warmly.

"Mrs. Trent!" he murmured a few moments later, and had to take off his spectacles to clean the vapor clouding his vision.

She smiled, but already her thoughts had turned to her niece. "Was Candace really meeting Mr. Reynald in Squire Epsom's woods, do you think?"

"It would appear so," he replied, his own expression sobering. "His lordship did not see fit to relate that part of the story, but I will tell you this, wife. If Harry Reynald has been trifling with Candace, then he shall be made to do the honorable thing, brother of an earl or not. If necessary, I shall marry them myself." He replaced his spectacles and reached for his gloves and hat.

"Where are you going, sir?" she asked.

"To the Boar's Head Inn. I will settle this business with Lord Doncaster at once."

"Where have you been?" Thomasina demanded when Candace stepped into the door twenty minutes later.

"Why, to see Mrs. Bellweather—"

"Oh, Candace, Jasper told Mama and Papa *everything*!" Theresa cried. "Is it true you were meeting Harry Reynald in Squire Epsom's woods?"

"And is he really Mr. Croyden's brother?" her sister asked, excitement sparkling in her eyes.

"Not Croyden," Theresa corrected her. "Papa said he's Lord Doncaster." She turned to her cousin. "Did you know he's really an earl?"

Candace looked in confusion from one to the other. "Uncle Jonathan knows?"

"It is true, then?" Thomasina squealed. "Oh,

heavens, I could just die. To think that I danced with an earl—but what a slyboots you are, cousin, not to have told us the truth. What is his brother like? Is he handsome? Are you going to wed him? Papa said he will insist on it."

Candace stared at her. "Wed Harry? What on earth are you talking about, and where is Uncle Jonathan? I must try to explain—"

"He's gone to speak to Lord Doncaster," Theresa informed her. "He left as soon as Mrs. Fairgood recovered sufficiently for Jasper to take her home."

"Recovered?" Candace asked, feeling much as though she were in the midst of a bad dream.

Thomasina giggled. "She swooned when she found out Mr. Croyden is an earl. And do not feel sorry for her, because that was after she suggested you be sent away someplace where you could be properly chaperoned."

Candace, her mind reeling, closed her eyes for a moment. When she opened them again, both her cousins were still standing in the hall and staring at her with anxious faces.

"You are not going to faint, are you?" Thomasina demanded.

"Possibly," Candace murmured. "I do not understand anything. Please, tell me exactly what occurred—from the beginning."

They both started to chatter at once, but Thomasina, being the eldest, took charge. She told her cousin how Jasper and his mother had called, and demanded to see Mama *and* Papa. "Of course, we were simply burning with curiosity. Papa had come home quite unexpectedly, and he behaved most strangely all morning, and Mama was not herself, but no one ever tells us anything. So we slipped out and listened beneath the drawing room windows."

"Do swear you will not tell Mama," Theresa interrupted, "or we shall not say another word."

Candace promised, and gradually, with frequent interruptions, questions, and much giggling, finally heard the complete tale from her cousins. But she was still terribly confused. Apparently her uncle had lied to protect her reputation, but such behavior was so far out of character for him that she found it difficult to believe.

"After Mrs. Fairgood left, we had to hurry back to the sewing room, but we left the door open, and when Papa talked to Mama in the hall, we could hear almost everything," Theresa added.

Thomasina nodded. "That's when Mama told him she was going with him, because she said you are just like her own daughter, and if anyone was going to discuss your marriage, she intended to be present."

"Good heavens, I must stop them," Candace said as she headed for the door. "There has been a terrible mistake."

"Candace! You cannot go alone. Wait for Theresa and me."

Chapter 14

Almerick de Courtney, the fourth Duke of Cardiff, gazed disdainfully about the courtyard of the Boar's Head Inn. "Are you certain this is the place?" he asked the slight man at his side.

"This is where I followed 'em to, and if an' it's all the same to you, Your Grace, I'll be taking my money and going on my way."

Cardiff, his florid face twisted into a sneer, tossed him a bag of coins. "Go, then, you sniveling coward. Just remember—if I learn you breathed one word of this, I shall hunt you down and put an end to your miserable existence."

Samuel Boodles needed no further urging. He scrambled from the coach without even counting his coins. If it meant walking back to London, he would prefer it to traveling another mile in the duke's carriage. He'd had dealings with some swells before, but never had he met a toff as nasty-minded or as vicious as Cardiff. It was almost enough to make him feel sorry for Lord Doncaster.

"Well, what are you waiting for?" the duke demanded of Snelling, his most trusted servant. "Open the bloody door and let down the steps."

Moments later, preceded by the obsequious Snelling, bowing and scraping and in general making it well known that a gentleman of great rank was condescending to visit this out-of-the-way establishment, the duke swept into the Boar's Head Inn.

Phineas T. Marley greeted his arrival respectfully, but was not nearly as deferential as he might have been weeks earlier, owing to his standing on terms with Lord Doncaster, who, in his humble opinion, was a true gentleman and not at all high in the instep. When his lordship had informed him of the Duke of Cardiff's imminent arrival, and that His Grace was not paying a friendly call, Phineas had generously offered to dust the doorstep with the duke's bottom.

Damian, who felt he had done nothing to engender such fierce and protective loyalty, was quietly astonished. But he thanked Phineas warmly, and assured him that he actually wished to see Cardiff, and that if the duke should inquire for him, be certain to say that he was staying at the inn.

Mindful of his lordship's wishes, Mr. Marley showed His Grace to the taproom, apologizing for the lack of a private parlor. "However, I doubt you'll be finding it too uncomfortable, Your Grace, as we don't get much custom during the day, except for my Lord Doncaster, who generally takes his meals here."

"Does he, indeed?" Cardiff said, glancing about the crudely furnished room. "Well, I always supposed he had the taste of a plebeian."

"I beg pardon, Your Grace?"

"Nothing," Cardiff muttered, waving the innkeeper away. "Just get me a bottle of your finest brandy, and then see that I have privacy. Snelling,

214

wait outside and keep a sharp eye out for Doncaster. Alert me the moment he arrives."

"I do not believe that will be necessary," a deep voice said from the doorway.

Cardiff swung around. "So, you *are* staying here. I suspected my man had taken leave of his senses when he reported you were putting up at this ... this tavern. Against the ropes, Doncaster?"

Damian strolled in, appearing entirely at his ease. He walked around the table to where the duke was standing, then tossed his cloak carelessly across a chair. After straightening the ruffles at his wrists, he replied languidly, "Not at all, Your Grace, but I might wonder about you. Your persistence in following me would seem to indicate a need— almost a desperate need, one might say—for funds."

Cardiff flushed, but stood his ground. "Or one might say that I simply have an intolerance for gentlemen who don't make good their gambling debts. Inasmuch as neither **you** nor your brother has seen fit to repay a vowel vastly overdue, I felt I had little choice but to come collect it myself."

Paddy slipped into the room and took a position on the other side of Snelling. The duke's man, effectively boxed in between the groom and the innkeeper, protested loudly.

Cardiff glanced around, then back at the earl. "Reinforcements, Doncaster? I am surprised. Considering the nature of our business, I rather thought you would prefer a more private conversation."

Damian gestured with an open hand. "I have nothing to hide, but pray, continue, Your Grace. I believe you were saying you had to come collect Harry's vowel yourself."

"You left me little choice," the duke replied as he very carefully removed his driving cape. He carried a pistol concealed in the pocket, but unfortunately it was not loaded. Careless of him, but he'd thought he would have time to tend to that matter before meeting the earl. But there was still a chance force would not be necessary. Everything depended on whether or not Doncaster's annoying young brother had survived his wound.

With a pretense of unconcern, Cardiff asked, "Speaking of your brother, have you seen or heard from him?"

At that moment Harry, looking impossibly fit and healthy, stepped into the open doorway and grinned at Damian.

His brother smiled. "I believe I shall let him answer for himself. Harry, His Grace is concerned about the debt he claims you owe him. Tell me, were you really foolish enough to play cards with him?"

As Cardiff swung around and stared at him in helpless fury, Harry replied cheerfully, "His Grace challenged me, what could I do? But you need not worry, big brother—I have the money I owe him."

"I am sure Lord Cardiff will be as vastly relieved as I am. Sixty thousand pounds is a great deal of—"

"Sixty thousand? Good God, Damian, don't be a gudgeon. Even in my cups I would never risk that much. I owe him six thousand pounds—I may have been bosky, but I distinctly remember that much."

"Then it appears we have an insurmountable problem. His Grace presented me with a vowel, signed by you, for the sum of sixty thousand pounds."

"You didn't pay it, did you?" Harry demanded.

"I rather thought I would like a word with you first," Damian replied.

"So that's why you came chasing after me. I wondered—"

"Pardon me, my lord," Paddy interrupted, "but the duke there appears a trifle restless."

Cardiff, who had picked up his driving cape and swung it over his shoulders, was edging toward the door. He halted abruptly and snarled at the groom. "Get out of my way, you bloody fool. Do you realize whom you're addressing?"

"Eager to leave, Your Grace? And yet, I do not believe our business is concluded," Damian said coolly. "Are you in such dire straits you must resort to forgery?"

"You are insulting, Doncaster. That vowel is in your brother's hand—I cannot help it if he was too drunk to know how much he lost."

"Liar!" Harry shouted. "You'll meet me for that."

"Gladly," Cardiff retorted. "Name the time and place. I would be delighted to teach you a much-needed lesson, but I do hope you're more skilled with a sword than you are with cards."

Damian motioned to Phineas to guard the door, then turned to the duke with elaborate politeness. "I beg your indulgence, Your Grace, but allow me a moment with Harry." He drew his brother to one side, and quietly attempted to persuade him to withdraw his challenge. "I understand your desire to run Cardiff through, but I doubt your arm is sufficiently healed to fight a duel."

"Did Candace tell you about that?" Harry asked,

undaunted. "I knew you would find a way to get around her."

"Miss Stafford aside, I wish you would permit me to take your place with Cardiff."

Harry shook his head. "I cannot allow you to do that, Damian. You've fought enough of my battles." Grinning wickedly, he added, "Are you not always telling me I need to stand on my own feet?"

"I was afraid you would say that." As Harry started to step away, his brother drew his right arm back. With the lightning move that had drawn praise from Tom Cribb himself, Damian connected with Harry's jaw, and the younger man sprawled unconscious on the floor.

"How touching," Cardiff murmured. "And undoubtedly wise on your part, Doncaster. Harry would not last above two minutes against me, but I suspect he will not thank you for your interference."

"Perhaps not, but my brother is recovering from a wound to his shoulder—the work of your hirelings, I understand. I had a rather informative chat with one of them . . . Turk, I believe he called himself."

Cardiff flinched and his small black eyes radiated a hatred that had Phineas reaching for the pistol he'd tucked into his apron.

"Were you not curious what happened to your men?" Damian asked.

The duke shrugged. "Good help is so hard to find—not that I am admitting anything. You will never prove a word of this, Doncaster."

"I don't intend to try. I suggest we settle it among ourselves. Swords or pistols, Your Grace?"

Cardiff glanced around the room. The pint-sized

groom Doncaster employed had gone to tend to Harry, who was still sprawled on the floor, but the innkeeper was guarding the door and he had a pistol leveled on Snelling. They were trapped. He knew the earl to be a deadly shot, and with a nonchalance he was far from feeling, remarked, "Swords, then. I could use the exercise, but when I am finished with you, I expect to walk out of here without interference from your men."

Damian laughed. "If you are still able to walk, you may leave with my blessings—only I suggest you plan on a lengthy journey, Your Grace. France, perhaps, for I will ensure you are no longer received anywhere in England."

"I suggest you wait the outcome of our match," Cardiff replied as he removed his coat, then sat down to take off his boots. While Paddy fetched the matched set of Italian blades from Damian's room, Phineas directed Snelling to shove the furniture against the wall, clearing a space in the center. Harry reclined in peaceful oblivion beneath one of the tables, out of harm's way.

The Dowager Countess of Doncaster allowed John Siddons to hand her down from her carriage. "I suppose there can be no mistake," she murmured, looking with dismay at the Boar's Head Inn.

"There must be," Phipps, her son's valet, declared as he descended the steps. "His lordship could not possibly be comfortable in an establishment of this sort."

"Comfortable or not, that's his lordship's carriage," Siddons said, pointing out Damian's yellow curricle. "And, if I am not very much mistaken, that coach belongs to the Duke of Cardiff."

The countess paled slightly, but her steps never faltered. "Something is dreadfully wrong. His Grace could have no business here unless it is with Damian or . . . or Harry."

"Perhaps, my lady, it would be better if you waited in the carriage," Siddons suggested.

She shook her blond head and lifted her chin determinedly. "If my sons are in trouble, my place is beside them."

Knowing it was useless to argue, Siddons nodded to Phipps, who opened the door for the countess.

She was not very tall, but she marched inside with an air of imposing regality that commanded instant attention. Mrs. Marley, tending the front of the inn and under strict orders not to allow anyone into the taproom, took one look at the countess and immediately curtsied.

John Siddons stepped forward and, with his usual civility, said, "Good day, madam. We are seeking Lord Doncaster, whom we have reason to believe is putting up at this establishment."

Mrs. Marley, her mouth gaping open slightly as she continued to stare at the countess, nodded her head slowly.

Impatiently, Phipps demanded, "He is here, then? Please be so good as to inform him that Lady Doncaster wishes to see him at once."

"I should like to be obliging you, sirs, but his lordship left orders he ain't to be disturbed." Involuntarily, her eyes slid to the taproom door. A muffled shout penetrated the front room, and in the ensuing silence the clang of metal striking metal could be heard.

Siddons strode toward the taproom, but Mrs. Marley was closer and she planted her stocky body firmly in front of the door and folded her hefty arms over her chest.

"Now, look here, my good woman—"

"Wait, Siddons," the countess commanded, and laid a delicate hand on his sleeve while she appealed to Mrs. Marley. "Lord Doncaster is my son, and I have had the most horrid feeling that he is in some sort of dreadful trouble. If he is within, you *must* let me see him."

Mrs. Marley was deeply torn. She had promised his lordship that no one would get past her, but surely those orders were not meant for his mother. On the other hand, if he was fighting a duel, and she suspicioned he was, then no good could come from his being distracted. Sadly, she shook her head. "If you just wait a few moments, my lady, I'm sure he'll be wishful of seeing you, but I can't be allowing you in—not until he gives me the word."

"I regret you feel that way," the countess replied, then flinched as another shout penetrated the heavy door. She turned to the servants, and with unyielding determination ordered, "Siddons, Phipps, remove her, please."

Phipps, his Adam's apple bobbing, shuddered slightly, but stepped forward gamely. He reached for Mrs. Marley's arm, but was unprepared for the elbow that jabbed his stomach. He doubled over in pain as Siddons tackled the proprietress on the other side. She was ready for him and locked a strong arm around his neck, nearly choking him.

Phipps, recovering a little, tackled her from the rear, but was unable to get a firm hold on her massive figure. He half climbed on her back in an effort to pull her heavy arms away from Siddons.

The countess, taking advantage of the struggle,

moved swiftly behind the trio and threw open the door. Mrs. Marley lost her balance at the same moment and tumbled in, bringing Siddons and Phipps crashing down with her.

Damian, having just collapsed into a chair, looked up as the door flew open. His bloody shirt hung in tatters from where Cardiff's sword had ripped it open. He had several shallow cuts on his chest, a deeper one in his side, and a long, jagged gash on his left forearm. His breathing was erratic and sweat had dripped into his eyes, blurring his vision. He blinked twice at the unholy vision before him, then chuckled.

It hurt his lungs and the pain in his side increased, but the sight of the very proper Phipps and John Siddons, whom he had never known to so much as raise his voice, much less a hand in anger, tangled on the floor with Mrs. Marley in the most undignified sprawl imaginable was too much. Damian threw back his head and laughed aloud.

Phineas took one look at the trio and flushed a bright red. "Mrs. Marley! Your legs is showing!"

Paddy, crouched beneath one of the tables with Harry's head cradled in his lap, had an unrestricted view of the melee and chortled delightedly. "Phipps, old man, the lady's on our side."

The countess was not amused. Her angry blue eyes took in Damian's wounds and the bloody sword still clasped in his hand. The Duke of Cardiff, stretched on the floor at the feet of the large man she took to be the proprietor, was obviously badly hurt. His eyes were closed and one hand gripped his shoulder, but the blood seeped between his fingers.

Her gaze returned to her eldest son. Despite his

ghastly appearance, he seemed to be in no danger. Logic told her Harry could not be seriously injured, either, not with Damian so patently amused, but a trace of fear still lingered, and she demanded in an icy voice, "What is the meaning of this, Damian? Tell me at once, is Harry—"

"Egad, that sounds like Mother," a groggy voice moaned from the back of the room.

Louisa swung around in time to see her youngest son awkwardly crawl out from beneath a table. Except for a bruise on his jaw, he looked well enough, and anger quickly replaced the relief she felt. "I shall not ask what you were doing beneath that table, or with whom you have been brawling, but will say only that I find your conduct both childish and reprehensible."

"Lord, that's rich. Damian knocks me out and fights a duel, and you take me to task. I always knew you favored him over me."

"Keep a civil tone in your head when you speak to Mother, or I shall put you under again, bantling," Damian warned.

"Not a chance. If you hadn't caught me off guard—"

"Enough!" Louisa commanded, silencing both her sons. She turned to the door, where Damian's servants stood sheepishly next to the inn's proprietress. "Siddons, please tend to His Grace, and when you've done what you can for his wound, remove him from my sight. Phipps, see to your master."

"Yes, my lady."

"You, sir, are you the owner of this establishment?"

"Phineas T. Marley at your service, milady," the

brawny innkeeper said, executing a surprisingly graceful bow.

Louisa nodded. "My sons will recompense you for any damage they have caused. Please prepare a reckoning. If Lord Doncaster is well enough to travel, we shall be leaving within the hour."

The countess was about to address Mrs. Marley, when an oddly dressed little man, his balding head gleaming in the sunlight, and his thick spectacles riding on the bridge of his nose, stepped into the doorway. A plainly attired but respectable-looking woman stood just behind him. Louisa nodded at them. "If you are seeking the innkeeper, please wait outside."

"Forgive me, my lady, but I require a private word with Lord Doncaster."

"Let me guess," Harry whispered to his brother. "The good reverend?"

Damian, brushing aside Phipps's ministrations, managed to rise to his feet. "Reverend, Mrs. Trent, do come in. I should like to present you to my mother, Lady Doncaster, and this is my brother, Harry Reynald."

Jonathan nodded politely to the countess, but his attention focused on Harry. "So, you are the young rapscallion who has been meeting my niece in the woods? I am glad you are here, sir, for your conduct has sullied my niece's reputation beyond redemption, and I demand you behave in an honorable manner. You shall be married without delay."

"What nonsense is this?" Louisa demanded. "On what grounds do you base these outrageous allegations?"

"I wish it were otherwise, my lady, for it is not an

alliance I favor, but you may ask your son for the truth of the matter," Jonathan replied.

She turned to her youngest, her eyes pleading with him for reassurance. "Harry? Pray tell me there is some horrid mistake."

Looking decidedly uncomfortable, he tugged at his cravat. "I did meet her, Mama, but it is not what you think. I was wounded and Candace— Miss Stafford—patched me up and brought me some food. I probably owe her my life, but I cannot think that she wishes to marry me—"

"Whether she wishes it or not, it must be," Jonathan interrupted. "Her reputation is ruined, and you, sir, are responsible."

Louisa paled, but she moved to her son's side, and with her back held stiffly straight, and her small chin lifted, she faced the Trents. "My son has, in the past, behaved irresponsibly on more than one occasion, but to my knowledge, he has never trifled with a respectable girl—"

"Are you implying my niece is not respectable?" Emily demanded. "Let me tell you, my lady, that I raised my girls properly and never has a breath of scandal ever touched one of them!"

Damian, who had been strangely quiet, glanced toward the door. "Perhaps we should permit Candace to tell us what she wishes. Come in, my dear."

She blushed as all eyes turned in her direction, but her gaze went directly to Damian's. "You are bleeding, my lord."

Damian nodded and then, with a dramatic flair that easily rivaled anything Harry ever dreamed of, fell back into his chair. "My pardon, ladies," he

murmured weakly, "but I fear I am near to faint-
ing."

Candace flew to his side, gripping his hand
warmly in hers as she knelt beside his chair to survey the damage. Then, like a lioness defending her
cub, she rounded on the others. "Are you all run
mad? His lordship is grievously wounded, and you
stand chattering and not the least effort made to
assist him? Mrs. Marley, I will require clean linen
and a basin of warm water. Basilicum powder, too,
if you have it."

The lanky valet took umbrage. "I *was* tending
him, miss, but his lordship said as how it was the
merest scratch—"

"What I said was that the merest touch of your
hands was sheer agony," Damian interrupted, then
groaned as he leaned back in the chair.

"You fools," Candace muttered scathingly. "Take
your bickering elsewhere.

"My dear," Jonathan remonstrated, "I do not
think you realize how this man has deceived us. He
is no better than his brother, and I cannot allow
you to stay here alone with him."

"I will stay with my son and Miss Stafford," the
countess announced with considerable interest,
eyeing the girl tending her son. Damian had never
fainted in his life, and he loathed anyone fussing
over him. On the few occasions he had been hurt or
ill, it had been a major accomplishment to persuade him to allow a doctor in his rooms. She
glanced at Damian, his long legs stretched out, his
arms dangling limply at his sides, and his head
resting against the back of the chair. He opened
one eye and winked at her.

"Begging your pardon, my lady," Siddons said as

he assisted Cardiff to his feet. "But what should I do with His Grace?"

"Put him in his carriage," Harry ordered. "Where's that man of his?"

"He got away when ... uh, her ladyship came in," Phineas said, struggling to keep a straight face. "But his groom's still out there."

"I need a doctor," Cardiff protested, rousing from his dazed condition.

"Consider yourself fortunate you don't require a grave digger. If Damian hadn't taken my place, I would have run you through—and you have my word that I shall finish the job if I ever see your face in England again."

Cardiff bit back a retort. He was clearly outnumbered and in no condition to battle further, but his black eyes gleamed menacingly as he allowed Siddons to assist him out the door.

Harry turned to his mother, taking her hand in his. "I apologize, Mama. I know you find such behavior offensive, but the duke is—"

She squeezed his hand in understanding, but then looked startled. "Harry, where is your ring?"

"Ring?"

"The one your father gave you—the emerald. You always wear it. Harry, tell me you did not lose it."

Damian groaned, then reached into his waistcoat pocket, making a show of monumental effort. "I have it, Mother. Harry gave it to me for safekeeping." He tossed it to his brother, then slouched in his chair again. "Could we discuss all this later?" he asked, his voice sounding pathetically weak.

Chapter 15

All Damian wanted was a few moments alone with Candace, but it had proved exceedingly difficult. It seemed any number of people wanted a word with him. He had finally pretended to fall asleep, and Candace had chased everyone out except his mother. But even she, bless her, had taken the hint and, on the pretext of fetching more linen, left them alone.

Damian opened his eyes as he felt Candace's feather-light touch gently cleansing his wound. It was peacefully quiet in the room now, and he took advantage of it to watch her. She bit her lower lip as she concentrated, her green eyes dark with concern.

He repressed an urge to reach up and run a finger down the entrancing lines of her cheek. Instead, he breathed in the intoxicating scent of her, lighter than roses, more like the first wildflowers of spring.

As if sensing his regard, Candace glanced up. For a moment she gazed into his eyes. Then her lashes swept down, hiding the love for him, which she could no longer deny.

Sorely tempted to pull her into his lap, Damian

took a deep breath and tried to speak lightly, "Where is everyone?"

"Your mother and brother are with my aunt and uncle in Mrs. Marley's private parlor, but you need not concern yourself. I told Uncle Jonathan that I will not wed Harry under any circumstances."

"I am vastly relieved."

"Your groom is seeing to the horses," she continued, ignoring his interruption. "And Mr. Marley is just outside the door. Mr. Siddons volunteered to help Mrs. Marley in the kitchen, as everyone seems to be hungry, and Phipps is in your chamber bemoaning the deplorable state of your clothes. I must tell you, sir, that he was a great deal more concerned with your appearance than with your wound. He even wished to change your boots before I finished bandaging your arm."

"I trust you sent him about his business?"

She smiled. "I did, but I suspect the reprieve is short-lived. The man seems obsessed. He was muttering that he suspected you had used ale on your Hessians, and looked positively ill."

"You must forgive him, Candace. He is London bred, and such things carry undue importance with him."

"But not with you, sir?"

"If I am obsessed, it is not with a pair of boots, but with a pretty green-eyed—"

"Ah, there you are," Jasper Fairgood cried, striding into the room. "Your lordship, my mother sent me to invite you to dinner—why, you are wounded!"

"You are most observant, sir. Pray give my regrets to your mother."

"This is most unexpected," Jasper replied, look-

229

ing utterly confused. "She will be extremely disappointed."

"I am not vastly pleased myself. Do you think you could manage to shut the door on your way out?"

Jasper hesitated, the impropriety of the situation weighing on his mind. "I suppose it would be allowable, seeing as how Miss Stafford is to become part of your family—oh, do not look surprised, my lord. The good reverend confided in us this afternoon—and Mama is all admiration for the way Miss Stafford managed to save your brother's life. Of course, I knew when I saw them together that a match was in the making, despite her efforts to pull the wool over my eyes."

"Jasper, go away," Candace warned as she rose to her feet. "His lordship is wounded and cannot be bothered with such nonsense now."

He laughed, though it had a hollow ring, and wagged a finger at her. "Now, my dear, you must not refer to your wedding as nonsense. We are all very pleased for you, and though I once had hopes that you and I—but we shall not speak of that. Mama asked me to convey her best wishes should I see you, and I hope that you will remember to invite her to the wedding. She is most fond of you, you know, and would be sorely disappointed not to see you marry."

Damian rose to his feet and advanced on Fairgood. "Out. I fought one duel today, do not force me to another."

Jasper involuntarily backed toward the door. "Really, my lord, I was just conveying Mother's regards. There is no need to become—"

"Out," Damian repeated, forcing the younger

man to retreat, and as soon as Jasper crossed the step, he firmly shut the door. Then he turned to face Candace.

"You appear much recovered, my lord," she murmured, suddenly feeling nervous as he approached her.

"I am—no doubt thanks to your ministering touch. Indeed, I suspect I am as much indebted to you for my life as is my brother . . . perhaps more."

He was so close, towering over her, that she found it difficult to breathe normally.

"My lord, I—"

"Damian," he corrected her, and with a hand cupped beneath her chin, gently lifted her face so he could see her eyes.

"Damian, I . . . I do not think we should be alone in here. The others will—"

"You forget, my darling, your reputation is already ruined. Why wouldn't you agree to marry Harry?"

She gazed into his dark eyes, losing herself for a moment in their smoky depths. He stirred passions in her she'd not known she possessed, and she suddenly longed to feel the strength of his arms around her.

"Some people, like the estimable Mrs. Fairgood, consider Harry an admirable catch. Of course, she does not know him, but I am certain that even were she acquainted, it would not alter her opinion. Most females seem to find my brother rather charming. I take it you are not of their number?"

"Do not be absurd, sir. Harry is like a brother to me."

"I am delighted to hear it."

His voice was whisper-soft, its warmth wrapping

231

around her heart, but that was nothing compared to the emotions he aroused when he pulled her into his arms. She opened her lips to protest, but he captured her mouth with his own. She struggled for a second only, then surrendered to the heavenly ecstasy of his kisses. *Champagne*, she thought, feeling light-headed. He was like the finest champagne, intoxicating, muddling her senses, filling her with an inexplicable joy.

It was Damian who pulled back, then gazed tenderly down at her. "I knew from the first moment that you defied me, that you were trouble, Candace Stafford. But I also know I shall never have another moment's peace if you do not agree to marry me."

For a brief second hope spiraled, then came crashing down. "Damian . . . you must be feverish. We could not possibly wed. It would be a dreadful misalliance—your mother would not be pleased. You cannot have thought this through."

She tried to free herself from his arms, but he held her firmly. "I have thought of little else. As for a misalliance, I know your uncle thinks I am not good enough for you, and very likely he's right, but I do love you."

"Oh, Damian, do not be so foolish. You know I was thinking of your mother. She will never approve."

"Nonsense. She will come to love you almost as much as I do."

"But the scandal in my family—you know about my mother."

"We have our own scandals to live down. Don't forget Harry is my brother."

"I . . . I have no dowry—"

"And need none. Did I not mention I am extremely wealthy?" His voice was teasing, but when he felt her trembling, he hugged her close. "Candace, darling, none of the objections you have raised matter ... unless, of course, you do not return my regard, and yet I had not thought you indifferent to me. Candace? Sweetheart, don't cry. What have I said?"

She gazed up at him, her green eyes shimmering and her lashes wet with tears. "I tried—so hard—*not* to love you, but it is impossible."

He gently kissed the tears from her eyes, then claimed her mouth with a commanding urgency that left her breathless. Holding her as though he would never let her go, he murmured against her lips, "Is it settled, then? Shall I order champagne to celebrate?"

Her hands entwined in the dark curls at his neck, she kissed the corner of his mouth. "I adore champagne."

Neither noticed the door to the taproom open, then quietly shut again as Lady Doncaster backed from the room with a useless armful of bandages. It appeared her eldest son was quite recovered, and not at all in need of her assistance.

Coming in January 1996.

A new novel of love and intrigue
in Regency England from
Jeanne Carmichael

FOREVER YOURS

Lydia Osborne has had five London
Seasons and is juggling three suitors,
but this headstrong young woman
still hasn't chosen a husband. Then
Lydia's ex-fiancé, Justin Lambert,
returns to London after five years of
fighting in the Napoleonic wars
determined to win back her heart.
Can this stubborn soldier dispose of
the competition and melt Lydia's
hardened heart before it is too late?

Published by Fawcett Books.